"Hey, pretty lady," a deep voice said next to her ear

"Don't take your mask off, Momma," Minnie said. "Guess who's come to watch your act?"

Her heart sank. He'd spoken the exact words she'd imagined him speaking. And his husky voice sent chills down her spine. Truly, this cowboy was a player at the master level.

"Minnie," she said, her voice warning her daughter to remember the rules—no cowboys. "Go sit in the stands, please."

"Now it's just the two of us," he said. "Clever of you to think of a way for us to be alone."

She ripped off her mask, ready to dispel his overwhelming appeal. The huge grin on his face stopped her.

He winked, slowly and sexily.

Her breath caught inside her chest.

Oh, no. She'd tol

She'd told herself

And this man mig

ever met to keep

she could.

ABOUT THE AUTHOR

Tina Leonard loves to laugh, which is one of the many reasons she loves writing Harlequin American Romance books. In another lifetime, Tina thought she would be single and an East Coast fashion buyer forever. The unexpected happened when Tina met Tim again after many years—she hadn't seen him since they'd attended school together from first through eighth grade. They married, and now Tina keeps a close eye on her school-age children's friends! Lisa and Dean keep their mother busy with soccer, gymnastics and horseback riding. They are proud of their mom's "kissy books" and eagerly help her any way they can. Tina hopes that readers will enjoy the love of family she writes about in her stories. Recently a reviewer wrote, "Leonard has a wonderful sense of the ridiculous," which Tina loved so much she wants it for her epitaph. Right now, however, she's focusing on her wonderful life and writing a lot more romance!

Books by Tina Leonard

CATCHING CALHOUN
Tina Leonard

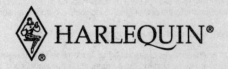

HARLEQUIN®

TORONTO • NEW YORK • LONDON
AMSTERDAM • PARIS • SYDNEY • HAMBURG
STOCKHOLM • ATHENS • TOKYO • MILAN • MADRID
PRAGUE • WARSAW • BUDAPEST • AUCKLAND

ISBN 0-373-75049-8

CATCHING CALHOUN

Copyright © 2004 by Tina Leonard.

This edition published by arrangement with Harlequin Books S.A.

® and TM are trademarks of the publisher. Trademarks indicated with
® are registered in the United States Patent and Trademark Office, the
Canadian Trade Marks Office and in other countries.

www.eHarlequin.com

Printed in U.S.A.

THE JEFFERSON BROTHERS
OF MALFUNCTION JUNCTION

Mason (38), Maverick and Mercy's eldest son—He can't run away from his own heartache or The Family Problem.

Frisco Joe (37)—Fell hard for Annabelle Turnberry and has sweet Emmie to show for it. They live in Texas wine country.

Fannin (36)—Life can't be better than cozying up with Kelly Stone and his darling twins in Ireland.

Laredo (35), twin to Tex—Loves Katy Goodnight, North Carolina and being the only brother with a reputation for winning his woman without staying on a bull.

Tex (35), twin to Laredo—Grower of roses and other plants, Tex fell for Cissy Kisserton and decided her water-bound way of life was best.

Calhoun (34)—Doesn't want the family mantle passing to him.

Ranger (33), twin to Archer—Fell for Hannah Hotchkiss and will never leave the open road without her.

Archer (33), twin to Ranger—Talking with a faraway woman in Australia by e-mail is better than having a real woman to bother him.

Crockett (31), twin to Navarro—Paints portraits of nudes, but never wants to see a woman fully clothed in a wedding gown saying, "I do" to him.

Navarro (31), twin to Crockett—Fell for Nina Cakes when he was supposed to be watching her sister, Valentine, who is carrying Last's child.

Bandera (27)—Spouts poetry and has moved from Whitman to Frost—anything to keep his mind off the ranch's troubles.

Last (26)—The only brother who finds himself expecting a baby with no hope of marrying the mother. Will he ever find the happy ending he always wanted?

To Texas Readers Dawn Nelsen, Sarah Procopio,
April Massey, Pat Wood, Cheryl Chan, Joanne Reeson,
Marcy Shuler, Melissa Lawson, and Denise Renae
Vellek. You ladies have meant so much to my
career and my life. Thank you so much.

Lisa and Dean—you are now fifteen and eleven.
I started writing when Lisa was two and a half years
old, and I went to my first writers' meeting when I
was pregnant with Dean. Many thanks to you both
for supporting my career, and for always being
proud of me. Mimi, thank you for believing in
my talent. Fred Kalberer and Kim Eickholz—
I was lucky when God gave me you.

Georgia Haynes—thank you for everything.

Last, but certainly not least, many thanks to
Stacy Boyd and Paula Eykelhof and all the
wonderful people at Harlequin who make
Tina Leonard a success. I have loved writing
this cowboy series for the best house—and
surely the most patient editors—in the world.

Prologue

The treasure lies within.
—Mason to his sons when they wanted to
know if there was such a thing as fairy dust
on butterfly wings and a box of Civil War
gold in the well on Widow Fancy's farm.

At exactly midnight, as a chilly November turned into a stormy, cold December, Mason Jefferson walked back into the main ranch house at Union Junction, wondering if he was ready to return home after being gone for so many months.

There were ten women in sleeping bags around the fireplace, where the fire had burned nearly to embers. His jaw dropped and he felt a sweat break out along the back of his neck. There were pretty faces, openmouthed faces, snoring faces, faces mashed into pillows.

Clearly nothing had changed around Malfunction Junction. Possibly the situation had worsened.

It gave a man pause about the reason he'd stayed

gone so long: Mimi Cannady, his next-door neighbor and wife to another man.

If women were so easily found around his fireplace, if they dropped easily into a man's life like blossoms from a cherry tree, if there were always many unattached females hanging around the Jefferson ranch, then why couldn't he get over the woman he *thought* he could only love like a meddlesome baby sister?

I came home too soon, Mason thought.

A crash sounded upstairs and a baby wailed. Mason closed his eyes. *I stayed gone too long.*

And after all his journeys he still had not a single lead on what had happened to Maverick, the father of the twelve Jefferson brothers.

"Hi, Mason." One of the women raised her head. It was Lily of the Union Junction hair salon in Union Junction. He and his brothers had helped her and her co-stylists set up shop in town, after Delilah Honeycutt had to let them go from the salon in Lonely Hearts Station.

"Hey, Lily," he said. "Go back to sleep. Didn't mean to wake you." He jerked his head toward the ceiling. "Think I'll go scare my brothers and see whose baby they're torturing."

Lily smiled. "Welcome home." She put her head down and Mason saw her eyes close. Sighing, he headed up the stairs.

In the second-floor family room, there were five brothers and a baby. A sweetly chubby baby, maybe a year old, he guessed, from the three tiny blond curls on the back of her head and her consciously erect posture. The brothers were arranged in a semicircle, all of them flat on their chests staring at her as she stared back at them. It was like a Mexican standoff, and the baby was winning, clearly bemusing her older companions.

It wasn't worth wondering whose baby it was. What mattered was that it seemed nothing had changed around Malfunction Junction. Still fun and games. "Howdy."

His brothers looked up and stared at him. Calhoun was the first to jump to his feet. "Mason!"

Mason tossed his hat onto the sofa. "I wasn't gone long enough for any of you to have a baby."

The other brothers halted, midrise.

"True," Calhoun said. "And this is not our baby, per se."

The baby turned her head to look up at him, and Mason felt his heart stop inside his chest. He would know that baby in a field of children; he could pick her out with ease. Fair, fine blond curls, big blue eyes that were her mother's, the sparkle of mischief in her expression as she'd enjoyed commanding the attention of her covey of "uncles."

"It's Nanette," Bandera said. "We're helping Mimi out 'cause she's been cooking for all of us and the ladies downstairs."

"Heat went out over the salon. Been out for three days," Last said. "Seemed the right thing to do to bring Lily and her crew here."

Crockett nodded. "They stood it as long as they could. We found out they weren't telling us, and had Shoeshine bring them over here in his bus."

Mason ignored his brother's blabbering, bending instead to scoop up Nanette and hold her to him. She didn't cry out at the chill in his fingers. Instead, she touched his face, patting it with curiosity, though he told himself she touched him because she recognized him.

"Been a long time since I held you," he murmured to her, so that his brothers couldn't hear. "You can sit up now. When I last saw you, you were just a tiny potato. I didn't know you would grow so fast," he said, nuzzling her. "You weren't supposed to grow up without me. I *missed* you." She patted his face again, and his eyes welled up with tears he wouldn't let his brothers see. "I shouldn't have left you."

The softness of her skin and her instant trust of him shattered his barely healed heart. Being gone hadn't solved a damn thing. He still loved Mimi, in a way he knew he should not. And he loved her child, the child he'd helped deliver, as if she were his very own.

In his heart, she *was* his very own.

Mason gruffly cleared his throat, aware that his brothers were uncomfortably silent. "What else did I miss?" he demanded.

The brothers glanced at each other. Last looked ill.

"How about we talk later?" Calhoun asked.

"We can talk now," Mason said.

"Not really," Calhoun said, glowering. "We've been amusing twelve months of dynamite. We're torn between using pacifiers, sippie cups, back rubs and guitar lullabies as good-luck charms to ward off the displeasure this child seems to feel at being out of her element. She doesn't like us, and quite frankly, we're beginning to wonder why babies aren't stored in pods until they ripen."

"We've had some ripe occasions," Archer said. "That one, delicate flower that she may be, can put forth some really ripe diapers."

"What we're trying to say, Mason," Bandera said, "is that we're tired. We're actually ragged. Let's get one thing straight from the start. You left. You took your bad moods and your broken heart and you deserted us. We've handled everything while you were gone. Now, we're of no mind to have you walk in here demanding answers."

"That's right," Crockett said, "we get first shot at Answer Number One."

Calhoun stood tall, crossing his arms. "Exactly. And *our* first question is, what in the hell do you think gave you the right to disappear like that?"

Mason stiffened. He'd had no right; it was just something he'd had to do. But he couldn't explain that to his brothers. What did they know of broken hearts, except when they were haphazardly doing the breaking?

Calhoun looked at him curiously. "Yeah, and while you're thinking of the answer, Mr. Wandering Foot, you might be interested to know that Mimi's filed for divorce from Brian."

Mason instantly went cold.

Chapter One

Nudes. Calhoun Jefferson loved painting nudes, he loved the color of bare skin and he loved women who were willing to get naked. That was a bounty for the eyes: women in the flesh—the different, varying skin tones that harmonized with the female personality. Dark, light, medium—he loved all the colors under the sun.

Particularly nude.

Some men saw heaven in a sunset. Some found God in the ocean's waves and secretive depths. "Ah, for me, it's the color of a nipple shadowed against the velvet of a rounded breast, the shades contrasting and yet complimenting, so tantalizing in hue," Calhoun explained to his brothers.

"Oh, God," Last said on a moan. "He's been to Hooters again."

"I have not," Calhoun said, indignantly slinging a saddle over a wooden rail. "I'm trying to explain my latest work of art to you undercultured dunces. I'm calling it 'Hues from Heaven.'"

"I feel more cultured already," Crockett said. "And my IQ has risen commensurately."

Calhoun sighed. "I'm heading over to Lonely Hearts Station for the rodeo. Anybody interested in going?"

"What for?" Archer asked. "Wait a minute, are you paintin' hooves again?"

Calhoun stood straight, staring at his brothers. "It just so happens that, this time, I'm entered, thank you very much."

"Entered as what?" Bandera asked. "Rodeo clown?"

"Rider," Calhoun said, deciding he wasn't going to let his brothers' jiving get to him. He had a mission today, and that was to advertise his afternoon art showing of first-class nudes by riding in the rodeo.

Of course, his show wasn't anything he wanted Mason to know about. Or his other brothers. They simply did not understand his love of artistic nudity.

"What I just can't get," Last said, "is if you like nekkid women so much, why don't you just get you one? We got about ten sleeping in our house this week, if you were too scared to notice. Just a set of jammies or a big sleep shirt between you and heaven's bounty. I say, pick one already."

Calhoun felt heat color his neck and rise up under his hat. "Have you been too *scared* to tell Mason that you have a woman living at the ranch who's expecting your child?" he asked, his tone deliberate and mild.

Every brother went still. Not even a jaw moved as they stared at Last.

"He just got home yesterday," Last said. "And he's been hiding from Mimi. I think I'd better give him a few more days to settle back in."

His point made, Calhoun walked from the barn. He wasn't scared of women! He revered women. And that was his brothers' problem, one of a thousand. They didn't understand that a man didn't necessarily have to sleep with his passion.

Of course, it was nice when he could.

But sleeping around had gotten some of the brothers married lately, and one of them was now expecting a child. "I'm figuring on keeping my jeans zipped, a lesson no one else around here seems to want to learn," he muttered, getting into his truck. "Broken hearts, babies, wedding rings—I'd say that nude women on canvas are a helluva lot safer than women in the flesh."

OLIVIA SPINLOVE knew about broken hearts and broken homes. She knew about cowboys and broken promises. She also knew about breaking bad patterns—and when her children, Minnie and Kenny, dragged the long, lean, hotly handsome cowboy toward her, Olivia defiantly crossed her arms over her chest.

"Hello," she said, her voice chilly. "I must apologize if my children have been bothering you."

"Not at all, ma'am," he said, lifting his hat and showing a toothy grin. "I find them charming."

"We got lost," Kenny said.

Sure they did, Olivia thought. They'd been raised on the rodeo circuit. They knew where their grandfather was and where the trailer was. "Thank you for escorting them back to me," Olivia said. "Sometimes they can be quite the handful."

"No, we're not," Minnie said. "We're angels." And she grinned up at the cowboy.

Olivia shivered. "Excuse us." She took the children by their hands and led them back to the trailer. Once inside, she sat them on the bed. "Minnie, Kenny," she began, "no. No, no, no."

The children looked at her woefully. "We need help," Minnie pointed out. "Grandpa's getting too old to do the act."

They were speaking of Grandpa Barley's knees being too arthritic to allow him to jump in and out of barrels these days. Olivia knew the kids were right, but that didn't mean they were going to interview cowboys at every rodeo in the United States until they found one suitable for their act.

"Your grandfather is fine, for now," she told them. "Please don't worry so much." She hugged them to her. "Really. It's going to be fine."

"How?" Minnie asked. "How is it going to be fine when we don't have an act?" Her large eyes were too old for her nine years and too worried. So little childish spirit lingered in Minnie's gaze.

Olivia smiled at her daughter, kissing her forehead. "Trust me, it's going to be fine."

Kenny began to bite at a hangnail. "It's not fine. I could get in the barrels, and Gypsy could find me instead of Grandpa."

How could she explain to him that Gypsy and Grandpa were a team, and that teams couldn't be broken apart? Once one member of the team no longer worked, the other went to pasture, too. At least in this case. Barley and his Gypsy were a horse and a man who could not be separated. *Tough old Dad,* Olivia thought. *And tough old horse.*

The two had always worked together to feed and take care of her family.

"Here's the deal," she told the kids. "I have to go ride Gypsy in a bit. If you promise not to 'interview' any more cowboys for Grandpa's job, I'll let you go watch the bull riding. If not, you can stay inside the trailer and do some math charts and spelling. I know you love to study, but I heard that there was going to be a superspecial bull tonight." She lowered her voice with excitement. "And no cowboy can stay on. It's a bounty bull. Mean as a three-headed rattler."

"Whoa!" Kenny breathed. "I gotta see that!"

"Me, too." Minnie slid off the bed. "It's a deal. No more cowboys tonight, Mom."

"Ever."

"Okay," Minnie said, giving out the promise at least, Olivia figured, until tomorrow. "No more cowboys."

"Good. I'll see you after the events. Kenny, stay with Minnie, and Minnie, you know the rules."

"Yes, I do," Minnie said, taking her brother's hand as they left. "No, no, no."

Olivia smiled as her children left the trailer. Someday she'd explain to them that their father had been a cowboy, one with a wandering heart. And though she loved her children dearly, the reason they were all in the shape they were in today was because Olivia had fallen under the spell of the Elusive Sexy Cowboy.

No more spells for her.

"WHOA," KENNY SAID, fifteen minutes later, having hotfooted it to the right to see the bull of which his mother had spoken. "Look at the size of 'im!"

Minnie nodded. "He's going to throw his cowboy into the next state."

Kenny giggled. "I can't wait. Cowboy's gonna look like a smushed grape by the time Bloodthirsty Black gets through with him."

"I like that bull's name," Minnie said thoughtfully. "The cowboy who stays on him wins a lot of money, cuz no one ever has."

"How much money?" Kenny asked.

"I don't know...." Minnie squinted her eyes at the bull. "A lot. That's what we need to stay out of trouble with—"

"The tax man," Kenny said helpfully. "Grandpa's always cussin' him."

"We need a lot of money," Minnie murmured. "Too bad you're not old enough to ride."

"I'd stay on 'im," Kenny bragged. "I'd stay on 'im like a gnat on his horn. Like spit in his eye. Like—"

"Hey, kids." A man's voice interrupted. "What's happening?"

Minnie glanced up into a pair of twinkling black

eyes. Friendly, and kind. Too nice for a bull like Bloodthirsty. She took a breath. "What's your name?"

"Calhoun."

"Are you going to ride Bloodthirsty Black?"

Calhoun nodded, amused by her question. "Yes, I am. Shouldn't you kids be with your parents?"

"Mom works with the rodeo," Minnie said bravely, thinking that the cowboy was awfully tall, the tallest one she'd seen in a long time. Maybe the biggest, too. "I've seen more rodeos than you'll ever see, cowboy."

He laughed. "Is that so, young lady? Well, then, I'll be on my way." Tipping his hat, he left the pair.

"Hey, I hope you win," Minnie called after the cowboy.

"If he doesn't, I'm gonna ride that bull," Kenny muttered.

"No, you're not," Minnie said. "Mom will never let you."

"And Mom said you weren't to size up any more, uh, marks," Kenny reminded her. "You looked like you'd seen a movie star when you talked to that cowboy. You got all goo-goo."

"That's what I'm doing wrong," Minnie whispered. "I'm looking for marks, when I should have been looking for goo-gooey."

"Huh?" Kenny stared at his sister.

"We don't need a cowboy to work for us, we need one for *Mom*."

They watched as the cowboy lifted a child, a little girl her own age, Minnie estimated, onto a pony.

"You mean, like a dad?" Kenny asked. "Grandpa Barley said he'd kick the bejesu—"

"Shh," Minnie said, "you're not to quote Grandpa when he goes south of good manners, Mom says. If that cowboy can stay in the saddle, we're going to find a way to drag him over to Mom. You can cry and I'll pretend to be lost."

"And you'll get in trouble," Kenny said. "Mom knows when you're, you know, looking out for her."

"Yes," Minnie said, "but Kenny, our life would be simpler with a man who can jump into a barrel. And that cowboy looks like he can handle barrels just fine."

"Maybe we should get Mom to watch him," he said. "Maybe she'd change her mind, although she'd probably say he was too big to…" His gaze wandered as he watched Calhoun walk to the other side of the arena.

"…to fit inside a barrel," Minnie finished for him.

"Yeah."

"Kids," Olivia said, walking to their side as they hung over the rail, looking out into the arena. "I'm about to start the act. You guys are going to be okay for another hour, right?"

"Yes," Minnie said. "Look at that man, Momma. That's the cowboy who's gonna ride Bloodthirsty Black."

Olivia glanced in the direction Minnie was pointing.

"He's very tall," Kenny said. "I don't think he'll be able to stay in the saddle."

"But he looks like Antonio Banderas," Minnie observed. "In that movie we weren't supposed to be watching when you fell asleep, Momma? Antonio could do *anything*."

"Let's all stick to G-rated movies from now on," Olivia murmured, her heart beginning to beat faster as she watched the cowboy walk. He did have a saunter to him, a loose swagger of confidence that caught the attention of every woman in the arena.

Then he turned around to wave to her children, and Olivia's heart sank deep inside her chest.

He's gorgeous.

Chapter Two

Too gorgeous to be anything but trouble in spades, she decided quickly. "Come on," Olivia told Minnie and Kenny. "Come watch Gypsy and Grandpa."

"No, thank you, Momma," Minnie said. "We want to see this man. I think he can stay on if he's been doing his cowboy calisthenics."

Olivia frowned. "What are those?"

"The ones you do in front of the TV every morning," Kenny said. "With the lady in the tight swimsuit who always smiles real big and says 'You can do it!'"

Olivia shook her head. "Those are not calisthenics. And that's not going to be a cowboy after he gets tossed and stomped."

"I think he's gonna win the big prize," Minnie said. "Calhoun, you can do it!" she called loudly.

The cowboy grinned at Olivia, touching the brim of his hat with two fingers in a roguish salute. She gasped and drew back. "You two come with me."

"Mom," Minnie said, "you wanted us to watch this. You wanted us out of your hair while you did the act. We're not going to try to get you to talk to him. We just want to see what he can do."

"It's Bloodthirsty Black," Kenny reminded her. "Mean as a three-headed rattler. We can't miss him!"

Olivia sighed, caught by her own sales pitch. "I wasn't trying to get you out of my hair. I thought you would enjoy seeing bull riding more than you'd enjoy an act you've watched a thousand times."

"Well, we are." Minnie gave her a squeeze around the waist. "We're fine. Don't be so worried about us."

Worry was her first and middle names where her children were concerned. But she'd been outmaneuvered here, though the cowboy didn't appear to have much on his mind other than his impending trip to the E.R. Olivia gave both her children a hug, then happened to glance toward the chute again. The cowboy was sitting on the rail, watching them with a grin on his face.

She had never seen a sexier cowboy in her life.

Her skin crawled, itched and tingled.

"Have fun," she said. "No talking to cowboys!"

"We won't," Kenny said. "Maybe just an autograph or two."

But Olivia had walked away, not hearing his last words. She couldn't stop thinking about shaggy long black hair, full smiling lips, and predatory black eyes that said *Hey, pretty lady,* even from a distance.

Wolf.

And she'd seen it all before. Maybe not in such a sinful package, but still, that cowboy wasn't going to sing her a trailside good-night tune.

SO THE TWO LITTLE rodeo urchins had a cute-as-a-bug mother, Calhoun mused. And no father watching over the family, apparently. The little girl hadn't said anything about a father in the rodeo when she'd mentioned her mother. He knew all the cowboys hanging around the stalls, and he'd never seen this particular family before. He wondered where they hailed from.

Shaking his head, he tried to focus on what the cowboys were saying about Bloodthirsty tonight.

Two little faces watched him intently.

Sighing, he thought about his art exhibition. The urchins' little mother would make a nice painting. He wondered what color her nipples were. Were they the shade of her lips, which had been a nice blush, or the deeper brown of her hair underneath the blond highlights? He loved nipples—they added an element of surprise. You never knew what color they would be. A lot of other things on a woman made sense; you could figure them out in advance. But nipples were dependent on the shading of the body, individual and unique to every—

"Cowboy, have you sent your brain to space?" someone called. "Earth to Calhoun, earth to Calhoun."

"Very funny." Calhoun slid off the rail. "I was thinking up my strategy."

"Really," another cowboy said, pinning Calhoun's number on the back of his vest. "From the stupid look on your face, we thought maybe you were daydreaming."

"About women," someone else said, and everyone laughed. "Sex-dreaming. About all the women who are going to want you after you tame this bounty bull."

"Nah, sex was the furthest thing from my mind," Calhoun said, lying through his teeth. "All my attention's on Bloodthirsty Black."

Except that small piece that had leaked out for a moment of fantasizing, Calhoun thought, glancing toward the children who watched his every move. It was so unlike him to find a woman in the flesh who stayed in his thoughts longer than his paintings did. Dang, he was going to have to be careful around those children. They had a smokin' hot mama—and that was the last thing he needed to be fantasizing about. There were too many surprise kids who had recently turned up in the Jefferson family tree.

He wasn't planning to add a branch. Or even a couple of twigs.

"You can do it!" he heard a little voice call.

"Cheering section?" someone asked.

"No." Calhoun turned to look at the children briefly. "Who are they?"

Everyone stopped what they were doing to stare at him.

"Barley's daughter Olivia's kids. Barley the rodeo clown. Tough character, Barley Spinlove. No one except a brainless wuss would ever think about dating his daughter, or marrying into Barley's family."

"Barley used to date Marvella," someone else explained. "Think he married her, but it didn't last long."

"And that's a bad reference right there," Calhoun said.

Marvella had a tough enough rep of her own. The owner of another bounty bull, Bad Ass Blue, *and* the Never Lonely Cut-n-gurls Salon in Lonely Hearts Station. Everyone had had a run-in with her at one time or another.

"Barley makes it known that he wants no part of a smooth-talking cowboy hanging around his daughter—she's got two kids from just that same incident. Cowboys can't be trusted—and Barley doesn't differentiate between us. We're all bad as far as he's concerned. None good enough for Olivia and his grandkids."

"Uses himself as an example of why women ought not date cowboys," someone else offered, and everyone went back to whatever they'd been doing.

"Great," Calhoun said. "Guess that means I won't be painting her." Or getting her clothes off. Or going out with her. And marriage was definitely out.

Marriage? Why had that thought floated through his brain?

"Of course anyone with a half cup of sense knew Olivia's marriage wasn't going to last. She married a first-class jerk, but that doesn't mean anybody else is going to get a chance," a cowboy muttered.

Calhoun looked up at the four faces staring at him. "Oh, don't tell me," he said. "I'm standing in the middle of the Olivia Spinlove Fan Club."

"It's Members Only," one of his buddies said

glumly. "Outsiders Not Welcome. So you have a better chance of staying on Bloodthirsty Black than you do of ol' Barley letting you take a walk with his daughter."

For some reason, Calhoun thought as he tugged on his creased, well-worn leather riding glove, that challenge just made him determined to be the one who took Olivia Spinlove for a moonlight stroll.

IN ACTUALITY, that stroll would have to be postponed.

Calhoun limped from the arena after Bloodthirsty tossed him to the ground with a flare of outstretched hooves and a ha-ha! attitude. He took stock of his body after he eased onto a barrel in an abandoned stall. Spleen rearranged, armpit felt loose, knee seemed dicey—perhaps a cranial dislocation. Damn, he was seeing stars.

"You okay, cowboy?" he heard a worried child ask.

And his two new friends seemed to be anxious to stick to him like gum on a boot heel. "I'm fine," he gasped out. "You two run along."

The girl looked at him curiously. "You don't look fine. You look like you might need a cup of hot tea. That's what Momma always gives us when we're not feeling 'up to par.'"

He groaned. "Well, now," he said, stripping off his glove and swallowing a pained groan. "I'd have to say I'm about three strokes shy of par."

"Not your best day," the boy said. "You'll play better another time."

"There won't be another time." Calhoun wished they'd go find another time in the next county and leave him to his busted pride. "Hey, you kids beat it for now, okay?"

With some guilt, he watched the little boy's eyes fill with tears.

"Oh, come on," Calhoun said grumpily. "You can't expect me to be friendly right now. My tongue's lodged somewhere behind my ears and my teeth seem weirdly disconnected."

"Kenny just wants an autograph," the little girl said, her tone mildly reproachful. "At least you *tried* to ride that bull, and that oughta be worth getting an autograph from you. So we can say we met the cowboy who *tried*."

Calhoun perked up. "An…autograph?"

The boy nodded, his eyes round and huge with either adoration or hope.

Calhoun's chest puffed out a little with male pride. "No one's ever asked me for an autograph before."

"You stayed on for three seconds," the girl said. "Kenny's easily impressed."

"Hmmph." Calhoun gave her an assessing eye. "You're too young to be sarcastic."

"Sarcastic?" Her eyebrows raised.

"Never mind." He scribbled his signature on the number he'd been wearing and gave it to Kenny, who seemed astonished over the gift. The little boy clutched it to his chest as if he feared Calhoun would change his mind and take back his number. "Now what? Don't y'all have someplace to be?" He eased himself into a different sitting position, wondering if he should take off his shirt to inspect his rib cage when there was a young lady about.

Probably not.

"Well, since the show's over," Minnie said, "we should go watch Gypsy find Grandpa in the barrels. Wanna come with us?"

Kenny's face beamed at him when he heard his big sister's offer. "Uh—" Calhoun began.

"You don't want to miss what Gypsy can do," Minnie bragged. "Mom's a great rider."

He perked up at the word "Mom." What the heck. At the end of every bull tossing should be a pretty woman. And he had a couple hours before the art showing. "Sure. I've got nothing better to do."

"Can you stand up?" Minnie asked. "'Cause we can help—"

"I can stand!" Calhoun insisted, annoyed that the kids thought he was so flimsy. "Now look, you two ragamuffins don't try to work me over, okay, because I know what you're up to."

Minnie blinked her big, innocent eyes. "You do?"

Satisfied, he nodded. "Yeah. I do. You want me for your mom."

The children stared at him.

"Grandpa said he'd kick the bejesu—" Kenny started.

"Shh! You're not supposed to say that!" Minnie reminded him. She looked up at Calhoun. "Cowboy, we want you to hide in a barrel. And that's all we're looking for."

Calhoun blinked, then narrowed his eyes. "Hide in a barrel? Do I look like the kind of stuffingless cowboy who needs to hide in a barrel?"

"From the way you ran from Bloodthirsty Black, we think you've got what it takes," Minnie said earnestly.

"Now, look," Calhoun said, pretty certain now that he was getting railroaded, "just because I said you were too young to be sarcastic doesn't mean I don't know when you are."

Kenny looked at him sorrowfully. "You don't want to be in our act? It's lots of fun." He got big tears in his eyes. "I told Mom I'd do it, but she said no. She said Gypsy goes out to pasture when Grandpa does."

They stared at him solemnly. Sighing, Calhoun eased to his feet. "You know what? You two are kind of strange. But I'm from the original House O' Strange, so I'll go along with the game for a couple hours. I've got nothing better to do." And if it meant getting a second look at Olivia Spinlove, then a man could do worse with his time.

THE GAME THAT BARLEY and Gypsy played was basically hide-the-pea-under-the-shell, only they used Barley and a barrel. Audiences were thrilled with the hide-and-go-seek game between Grandpa and Gypsy, because Gypsy wore blinders and therefore seemed to really be able to figure out where Grandpa was hiding, even when Olivia made Gypsy go over to a child in the audience, giving Grandpa a chance to hurriedly switch barrels. Gypsy always went to the new barrel immediately, making the audience laugh as she reached in with her nose to check for him. On command, she would whinny very loudly, as if to say, Ah-ha! She could push barrels over with Barley in them, and she could kick them, making Barley yell "Ouch!" much to the delight of the children in the crowd.

Olivia was responsible for the gag running quickly and smoothly. She herself wore a mask over her eyes, so that she couldn't "cue" Gypsy to the correct barrel.

Sometimes Gypsy pretended she didn't know where he was, and Olivia would ask the kids to "help" Gypsy find Grandpa. While they called out answers, clowns would run through the audience giving fresh apples to kids who participated, even if they just pointed a finger. Most of the time, every child ended up with a pretty apple.

And at the end, Grandpa did a sparkler show while sitting on Gypsy, his arms pinwheeling in figure eights and lasso motions as the children watched in amazement.

Then every child who wanted to could pet Gypsy.

Olivia adjusted her mask, thinking that it was sad that the show would be over at the end of this school year. In fact, this was the final time they'd perform in the south. Lonely Hearts Station had been one of the few places where they hadn't performed. Barley had ditched the town many years ago, after Marvella and he had a row.

Olivia suspected he'd never gotten over Marvella. He really was an old softie, though he had a reputation for being mean. They'd probably never get back together, but first flames often burned in the memory. Still, life went on.

She waited for her cue to bring Gypsy into the ring.

"Hey, pretty lady," a deep voice said next to her ear.

"Don't take your mask off, Momma," Minnie said. "Guess who's come to watch the act?"

Her heart sank. He'd spoken the exact words she'd imagined him speaking. Truly, this cowboy was a player at the master level. "Minnie," she said, her voice warning her daughter to remember the rules—no cowboys.

The man stopped Olivia's fingers as she raised her hands to take off the mask. "I like it," he said. "Mysterious women are quite interesting."

"I'm not interested in being mysterious for you," she snapped. "Kenny, Minnie, go sit in the stands, please."

"'Kay, Mom. See ya, cowboy," Minnie said.

"Now it's just the two of us," he said. "Clever of you to think of a way for us to be alone."

She ripped off her mask, ready to dispel his over-enthusiastic appeal, when the huge grin on his face stopped her.

He winked, slowly and sexily.

Her breath caught inside her chest.

No, no, no, she'd told the kids about cowboys. And *no* she'd told herself. This man might be the best reason she'd ever met for saying no to cowboys.

"Your kids said I shouldn't miss the show," he told her, his husky voice sending chills down her spine. "My name's Calhoun Jefferson, of the Union Junction ranch. Better known as Malfunction Junction," he said with a grin.

"Why do I find that easy to believe?"

"Because you can tell I'm a man of my word."

Olivia raised an eyebrow. "Cowboy, you are full of yourself."

"And you find it strangely appealing." He patted Gypsy under her mane, right along her neck where she liked it best.

"Is that what all the ladies tell you?"

He grinned. "What ladies?"

She rolled her eyes and snapped her mask back on.

"Oh, come on," he said softly, "unbend a little. A little mama like yourself ought to enjoy some harmless flirting. It's nothing more than keeping a lonely cowboy company. And you're not exactly hard on the eyes, you know."

"Flattery will get you nowhere, Mr. Jefferson. And please refrain from buttering up my kids."

"On the contrary. They buttered me up, put me on a plate and brought me to you for a friendly snack."

She flicked Gypsy's reins. "Friendly snacks have a way of putting weight on a woman, cowboy, and I'm on a special snackless diet. Goodbye."

Olivia moved Gypsy forward, away from Calhoun. Calhoun! She might have known he'd possess an unusual name. He'd said he was harmless, but they all said that.

After tomorrow night's show, she would round up Minnie and Kenny and head out of Lonely Hearts Station. Time was not on her side. That darn cowboy was reading her mind like a newspaper, and he knew full well she was attracted to him.

It wouldn't hurt to take that bold confidence down a peg. Turning, she lifted her mask. "Mr. Jefferson."

He grinned, obviously thinking his charm had won her over. "Call me Calhoun."

She nodded. "Calhoun, did you beat the buzzer?"

"No, ma'am. I must admit I did not."

"Ah." She pretended great interest in her mask before looking back at him. Her voice sexy, she said, "How long did you last?"

He grinned. "Three seconds. Generally, I last as long as I need to, though."

Her lips flattened out as she realized he was on to her wordplay, and his confidence wasn't dented a bit.

"Yes," he said expansively, "they call me Countin' Calhoun. Three is usually my minimum. I'm disappointed cuz it'll bring down my average of nine."

"Nine seconds?" She blinked.

"Oh, no, ma'am. Nine…well, I'm sure you can figure it out."

She felt the blush hit her cheeks like summer's heat. Her hands snapped Gypsy's reins of their own accord, and she rode stiffly away from his laughter.

Blast him. Now her mind was racing! Nine hours,

nine orgasms, nine what? "I would *love* to know," she grumbled to herself. "Braggart!"

She hadn't enjoyed making love with her husband. Truthfully, she had been no proper wife, because if there had been a night she could avoid even kissing him, she did. Maybe she'd only gotten married to have children.

As much as she loved her father, his stranglehold on her younger self had been too much for her. In her heart, she'd made peace with the fact that most likely her teenage rebellion had blossomed into two children. It didn't matter now, but she knew well enough from her marital experience that she was not a good wife.

So it really didn't matter what Calhoun was counting—though she'd never before heard a man so proud of his numerals.

Chapter Three

Calhoun was impressed with Olivia's act—the one where she pretended she wasn't interested in him even more than the one with Gypsy, Grandpa and the barrels. He left the show, heading to his truck.

Olivia's no-sizzle charade intrigued him. Never had he seen a lady with more sex appeal trying so hard to hide her light under a bushel basket, as the old-timers used to say. She wouldn't even let loose with a smile for him—and that told him a lot.

It told him Olivia was chicken. He'd caught her checking him out, and she didn't mind dueling with wordplay, so the passion was there. She'd simply turned her sex switch to the Off position.

A better man might find a way to flip that switch back on.

It would be a fun chase, and he had no doubt she'd give him the run of his life, which he would enjoy thoroughly. Yet it seemed to him that was probably how his brothers had ended up at the altar—thinking with their Sex Switch Fix-It Kits.

He had his nudes to keep him company, and he'd have to be satisfied with that.

"Calhoun?"

The voice stopped him before he took the tarp off the truck bed. He turned. "Olivia?"

She blushed. "Can I talk to you?"

She could talk to him. She could walk with him. She could— "Sure. What's up?"

Glancing around, she said, "It's a private matter."

Oh, yeah. His favorite kind. "Well, we could sit in my truck, or we could walk to the tearoom, or—"

"Your truck is fine. Thanks."

She hopped into the driver's side and slid across the seat before he could open the door for her. Dang, he'd never had a woman so eager to spend time alone with him. He shut his door and waited expectantly.

"I won't take up much of your time," she began. "I must ask you to stay away from my children as much as possible. I know they've been seeking you out, and I'm going to talk to them about that, but in any case, I'd appreciate your help with this."

Now that wasn't the prelude he'd been hoping for. His spirit dimmed a bit. "Why? Have I upset you somehow?"

"No. It's complicated, actually, and forgive me for not wanting to explain more, but it would just be best."

He narrowed his eyes thoughtfully. "For you, for me or for them?"

"For everyone."

Hmm. This lady was more afraid of her switch

than he'd thought. Tapping the steering wheel, he said, "Of course I will do whatever you ask."

"Thank you."

He nodded, sensing her relief. "Can I ask one question?"

"Yes."

"If we weren't attracted to each other, would I be getting this No-Kids-Zone request?"

She looked at him. "Cowboy, I never said I was attracted to you."

"You wouldn't say it, even if it were the truth."

Her lips formed a rosebud of disapproval. He made a mental note that this woman was darling even when she was annoyed, which was important. Some women were downright scary when they were annoyed. A man factored in facial expressions when he was getting to know a woman. An artist such as himself was particularly attuned to the range of expressions each female possessed.

She might be affecting his barometer of sexual attraction, but this female's needle gauge was hovering right around the Back-Off-Buddy range.

"Thank you for understanding about the children," Olivia said, opening the truck door. "They are always scouting for men. Although I will say that they're a little more enthusiastic about pitching you."

"Thanks. I think." He let her get out of the truck, though he was sorely tempted to take her fragile little wrist and pull her back inside for a goodbye kiss that would make her think ten times before she shut that door in his face.

However, the combination of her switch turned off and her lips budded with displeasure signaled he should keep his tendencies to himself for the moment. He also sensed sweet talk was not the way to crack her defenses.

Damn, she was a puzzle.

"I'm good with puzzles," he murmured out loud.

"I beg your pardon?" She halted before shutting the door.

"Oh. Never mind. Sorry."

"It sounded like you said 'I'm good with puzzles.'"

"No."

She looked at him suspiciously. "Have a good afternoon."

"Goodbye," he said, his meaning clear. Might as well join the game of hard-to-get since that seemed to be her seduction of choice.

But she closed the truck door without even a moment of regret or coyness, and Calhoun realized she really wasn't up to anything more than what she'd said: asking him not to buddy up with her kids.

The whole thing hurt his feelings a helluva lot more than it should have.

So it startled him when she tapped on the driver's side window a few minutes later. It rattled him, he admitted, because he'd figured she was long gone with dust trails behind her. He opened the door. "Did you forget to spoon out the last chunk of my feelings?

Come back to play the last song as the lights dim at the bar and Calhoun goes home somewhat annoyed and depressed?"

Olivia blinked. "Why would you be depressed? You don't even know us."

He shifted, pushing his back against the seat cushion. "What am I supposed to do, Olivia, if I see your kids again? Walk on by?"

Her eyes opened. "The rodeo's only going on for one more night. After that, it won't matter."

"No, it won't—but, to be honest, I've never had a woman ask me to stop being friendly to her kids. And I will admit that it kind of sucks." He frowned. "I don't see what harm I've done."

"You haven't. It's very difficult to explain, Calhoun, but my children are sort of…thinkers. Worriers, if you will. And they try to manipulate their environment. In this case, the environment is you."

He really didn't know what to say to that much honesty.

She looked at him, and he could tell she was embarrassed.

"So you're saying I'm just a target for their attention?"

"Right. One in a long line."

Ouch. He didn't like to be in long lines anywhere, unless it was a cattle parade at the rodeo.

With a sigh, she said, "This isn't easy to say about my children. But I'm sure you can appreciate my position as a single parent."

"Sure. You don't want your kids scoping out potential fathers."

She frowned. "Fathers? I don't think that thought ever entered their mind. They have my dad as a father figure."

Hmm. He hadn't considered that. They did have a version of the classic nuclear family. "So what do they want from me?"

"The question is better posed as 'What do you want from us?' Because I think that's where the problem comes in."

He ran his hand through his hair and put his hat back on. "Look, I think my M.O. is pretty simple. I just want to kiss you. And if being friendly to your kids comes along with the package, I'm cool with that. They're a different sort of crew, but what you don't know, because you don't know me well enough, is that I'm kind of at home with strange characters."

"Kiss me?"

Her eyes were open with something like shock, or maybe alarm. Calhoun considered that. Clearly, kissing him had not crossed her mind. Pow! One more sock to the ole ego. Man, this woman had her sex switch permanently lodged in the Off position, and it would take a god of Herculean enterprises to move the damn thing.

"A kiss is not exactly asking you to jump off a bridge, you know," he said sourly. "Pardon me if I thought you might, you know, find me attractive.

Like I do you. Although you are getting on my nerves with your lack of response to my manly attributes."

She started to laugh. He thought it sounded more like nerves than amusement, though, so he decided to go with it. "Share the joke."

"I can't. There's no joke. Really. It's just that…you don't want to kiss me, cowboy. Trust me."

"I think I will be the judge of my sexual desire, thank you very much," he said. "But let me find out for myself so I can be honest with both of us."

Calhoun swept Olivia into his lap, just the way he'd been dying to do since meeting her, and he planted a kiss right on her lips. Olivia didn't move, probably from surprise, so he cradled her face in his hands and began a more gentle assault on her locked-down security position. Softly, he moved his lips against hers, then lightly ran his tongue across her lips before pressing his mouth against hers over and over again.

And everything in his jeans went straight to attention. He might have burst a seam somewhere. Yowza, this little mama smelled good, she felt great, and her mouth was made for his.

He could spend a lifetime kissing her.

Calhoun shoved her out of his lap. "You're right. I didn't want to kiss you."

She gasped, and then, to his everlasting surprise, she slapped him one across the face before whirling off.

Now, granted he'd been hit harder in his life, and

goodness knows, it had been more a whisk than a smack that she'd landed—but it was the intention that startled him.

The little minx. And he still had an erection—blast her curvy little rump that had heated his zipper as she'd sat in his lap. "I'm pretty certain she's annoying me," he muttered. "She tried to slap me, and I still have the itch to go after her. Where I come from, I know that would be considered a bad omen!"

Especially since he'd been fibbing to save his soul.

He *had* wanted to kiss her. And he wanted to do it again—soon.

THE WORST THING a man could tell a woman, Olivia decided, was that he didn't want to kiss her—after he'd insisted upon it. The arrogant cowboy! Once again, her theory about cowboys was proved true. The Elusive Sexy Cowboy was the most devastating thing that could happen to a woman.

He'd managed to tear apart the first budding of her heart without even trying.

Maybe not actual budding, she thought. Maybe just a scratching of new growth hidden beneath a winterized girdle of dormant seed, but she'd felt the stirring. Like a new plant turning toward the sun, she'd felt herself warming to Calhoun. A surprising ray of hope had lit inside her when he'd put his mouth against hers, touching her kindly and gently, awakening feelings she'd never known she could possess.

It had felt so wonderful to kiss him. He had no idea how much she'd delighted in finding that a man's kiss could give her pleasure instead of revulsion.

And then, he'd crushed her new growth.

He'd think twice before he tried to steal another kiss from her—and then insult her inexperience.

Crawling into the bed inside the trailer, Olivia slipped between her kids. They curled up next to her, as they always did, making her relax with contentment. Here was what mattered to her heart. Kenny and Minnie: the best part of her life.

At the other end of the trailer, she could hear her father snoring as he took his nap. Everything was in its place. In a little while, she'd take the kids to see tonight's fun. There would be face painting and art exhibits and other exciting things for them to do— and she was going to forget all about Calhoun and his effect on her.

She was going to forget everything except his kiss. That had been a surprise, making her tingle all over. Even if Calhoun was a bad thing for her, his kiss had been very good.

He need not ever know exactly how one simple kiss had changed her awareness of herself. Today, she felt as if life was starting all over again.

She was glad she'd slapped him for being a horse's ass, though.

"I SHOULD KISS HER AGAIN," Calhoun told himself when he saw Olivia and her kids wander into the exhibit pavilion that evening. "And then tell her I'd been tweaking the truth just a wee bit."

But she'd asked him to stay away from her kids because they were seekers of some kind. He frowned, wondering what they needed so bad that they had a habit of trolling for men. It didn't matter. Olivia was with her kids, and she'd asked him not to be friendly with them, so no kissie-kissie, duck-the-slappie for him tonight.

"Nice paintings," a man said.

"Thanks." Calhoun nodded. "Been painting all my life."

"You've done some beautiful work." The short cowboy had a little daughter with him, Calhoun noticed, and he hoped the child wasn't affected by all the nudes. She was pretty young, and she was busy with the cotton candy that was smudging her face with pink webs of sugar. Calhoun exercised his right to be friendly with the child. "Hey," he said, lifting the girl onto a barrel so that she could sit and eat her cotton candy—and be out of range of the paintings while her father shopped. "Keep my chair warm for me, would you, princess?" he asked.

She giggled and smiled at him, and Calhoun felt momentarily sad that he couldn't enjoy the company of Kenny and Minnie this way. They'd had a good repartee going—something he didn't expect to have with young children—and he was surprised to find that he missed them.

"DID YOU SEE THAT?" Kenny asked Minnie as they spied on Calhoun across the pavilion. "That little girl is shopping for Calhoun."

"I don't think so," Minnie said, making certain their mother's attention was on merchandise in one of the makeshift booths. "She has a father with her. Now if she had her mother with her, I'd say she might be shopping for him—"

"I don't see why we can't talk to him," Kenny grumbled. "He's nice."

"Yeah." Minnie certainly agreed that the cowboy was nice. So she understood Kenny's concern. They'd sort of chosen Calhoun for themselves. And they didn't like sharing, especially not with a little girl who was younger and cuter, who wore a pretty pink dress and white ankle socks with lacy edges, and who had blond ringlets and cotton candy.

Minnie's lips pressed together as she looked down at her overalls and scuffed shoes. Did she remember to use her hairbrush today? Momma always said she should, and usually Momma made sure of it, but to-night her mind had been elsewhere, and Minnie had taken advantage of that to slip out without brushing. Self-consciously, she ran her hand over her long hair, smoothing it, then spit on her hand to flatten down Kenny's hair.

"She's already got a father," Kenny said. "I want to go push her off that barrel."

Minnie stopped her spit adjustment of Kenny's bristly head. "She does seem to have everything."

Feeling badly for her jealousy, she glanced toward her mother, who had moved to the next booth. "Sometimes life doesn't feel quite fair."

"We need a father," Kenny said stubbornly.

"We have Grandpa."

"Yes, but if he's getting too old to jump in and out of barrels, then…"

Then what else might he be too old for? Minnie thought. Playing? Living? She glanced back over to Calhoun, then gasped as she saw him painting something on the little girl's plump cheeks. "Come on," she said to Kenny, "I can't see when we're this far away!"

"I CAN PAINT A WOMAN on a saddle for you," Calhoun said, "but I'm afraid it won't last."

"Still," the man replied, "my butt will be happy while she does, if you know what I mean. And it's probably longer than most real-life women last."

Calhoun held back a grimace. Rough as the Jefferson household could be, he was pretty certain a man didn't talk about naked women in front of a child.

"Let me see your unicorn, sweetie," he said, as he finished the last strokes of sparkly paint he was applying to her cheek. "It's almost as pretty as you," he told her, though he'd wager cotton candy would be dulling the sparkle in no time. The child seemed very impressed with her treat, and not as impressed with Calhoun's rendering on her face, but he figured with both of his customers happy, the world was good.

At least he thought so, until he saw two little faces

peering at him from behind an easel that held a large portrait.

"Thank you, sir," he said, pocketing the money he'd been paid. "I'll get on that saddle right away."

The man grinned, taking his daughter by the hand. "I can't wait to see what you can do."

Calhoun waited until the customer was gone, then glanced around. No Olivia. "Okay, you two, come on out."

They did, rather sheepishly. "What are you up to now?" he asked.

Minnie blinked at him. "I want a sparkly unicorn on my face."

"And I want a sparkly deer," Kenny said. "A reindeer. Like Santa has."

"Er—" Calhoun squirmed. How could he turn them down? And yet, he couldn't go against their mother's wishes. "Where is your mom?"

"Over there," Minnie said airily. "Don't worry. She won't want her face painted."

"Yeah. You can just do us." Kenny beamed.

Calhoun sighed. "You two are a pack of trouble, you know it? Your mother says I'm to stay out of your clutches."

Minnie nodded. "And we're not to bug you."

"Bug me?" Calhoun cleaned a paintbrush. "Bug isn't the word I'd use. And I don't think that was the word your mom used. Was it?"

"No." Kenny frowned thoughtfully. "She said we were not to take up your time. Which means 'bug.'"

Calhoun shifted as he thought through his dilemma. Should he tell the children to go away? That would hurt their feelings. He'd seen the look in Minnie's eyes as she'd watched him painting the little girl's face. He'd seen a lot in that moment. "Hey," he said suddenly, "what exactly is it you two want from me, besides some face painting? Tell the truth."

"We told you," Minnie said. "We think you'd make an awesome barrel act with Gypsy on account of how fast you can run. But," she sighed, "now Kenny's decided you'd make a better father."

Calhoun halted. "Father?" He glanced at Kenny.

The kids shrugged at him. "Maybe," Kenny said. "I'm thinking 'bout it."

Whoa. Olivia would freak if she heard her son say that! "Ah, okay. Here's the deal. This is my price for face painting."

The kids edged closer to him, eager to barter.

"I will paint one thing for each of you, but you have to promise me that you will never say to your mom what you just said to me."

They stared at him.

"Why?" Kenny asked. "We don't usually keep secrets from Mom."

"Trust me, this is a good one to start with." He patted Kenny's back. "Is it a deal or not?"

The kids nodded. "Deal. We won't tell Mom how fast you can run," Kenny said.

Calhoun squatted down to where they could look down into his face. "That wasn't it, exactly. Skip the part about looking for a father. That's not something she wants to hear."

Kenny sighed. "Okay."

Minnie stared at him. "We're not dumb, Calhoun. We know it'd never work."

After a moment, he nodded.

"I mean, there *are* other girls in the world, ones who wear pretty dresses and ribbons in their hair and who don't spit-comb their brother's hair," she said mildly.

He glanced at Kenny's hair with some interest. "Spit-comb?"

Minnie shrugged. "Works better than water."

"Hmmph." He took her small hand in his. "Just for the record, I'm the kind of guy who's more impressed by ingenuity than froufrou, okay?"

"Cowboy, I'm pretty smart because my momma homeschools me, but I don't know what froufrou means. And neither does Kenny."

Kenny shifted from boot to boot. "Can we start now? Before Mom finds us and drags us off for another lecture on how we're not supposed to be bothering Calhoun?"

Calhoun grinned. "Just remember what I said," he told Minnie. "One day you'll meet a guy who feels the same way I do about froufrou, and you'll know he's the one."

Minnie sat on the barrel, taking the little girl's place and feeling pretty good about it. "Maybe Momma would like you better if you spit-combed *your* hair," she commented.

Calhoun smiled and picked up his paintbrush. "Keep your head turned this way and don't glance at the paintings."

"We already saw them," Kenny said. "They're naked women. You must like naked women a *bunch.*"

"And you're going to paint a naked woman on a saddle for that man, to make his butt happy," Minnie said. "I guess that's what you mean by froufrou."

Calhoun looked at Minnie, with her honest eyes, her straight hair and her wide mouth, which was, co-incidentally, budded up into the same expression of disapproval he'd seen on her mother's face earlier. On Olivia's face he'd found it cute—but on Minnie's face, it was disconcerting. Olivia was right: her child was a worrier.

And her equally worried brother sat beside her, with eyes like Minnie's, only Kenny's had a deeper reservoir of sadness, almost like Charlie Brown, as if his world was never going to be quite right but he'd keep searching for the good in life anyway. *Catch 'em being good,* adults liked to say about children. In Kenny's watchful gaze, it was as if Kenny was waiting to catch Calhoun being good.

"You know," Calhoun said heavily, sitting down next to them. "I should paint you two."

"I want a deer," Kenny said, as Calhoun touched the paintbrush to his cheek.

"I meant, paint a portrait of you. Together."

Minnie watched over his shoulder as his hand moved deftly over her brother's face. "Why?"

"I don't know why. Change of pace, maybe." He'd never painted anything but nudes. Well, once in high school, he'd painted graffiti on the gym walls and gotten suspended for three days—after he'd painted the entire gym again, by himself, in a new coat of school colors. The school had suspended him, but it had been Mason who'd dragged Calhoun back to the school to tell them he wanted to make right what he'd done wrong.

Curse Mason, and curse Maverick's legacy of trying to instill rightness in all of them. It was almost like having a Goody Two-shoes gene one couldn't outrun.

"If you paint us," Minnie said, her voice colored with wonder, "paint me with a pretty dress and ribbons. My hair done right, and Kenny's lying down, not stuck up like a bird perch on his head. Okay, Calhoun?"

Calhoun stopped, his hand floating in the air, paintbrush suspended, as he realized what she was saying.

Minnie dreamed of a world she was never going to have, even if she was practical enough to know that her life with her family was better than the little girl's with the ribbons and cotton candy and father who wanted his butt to be happy. But still, she dreamed of adding more color to her personal portrait. She'd remodel Minnie Spinlove.

"Minnie and Kenny, what are you doing?"

Olivia's voice startled Calhoun. He turned to face

the mother of the children whose faces he was painting. She looked none too happy.

Before he could stop himself, Calhoun reached out and painted a big dot on Olivia's cheek.

She stared at him as if he'd lost his mind.

"Face painting," he said. "And we're obeying all the rules. They're paying customers, Ms. Spinlove. Scout's honor. Just like the little girl who was here before getting her face painted. Even ladies like to get their face painted. It takes them back to their childhood. Would you like your face painted?"

"No, thank you," Olivia said. "I will wait until you are finished, though. I suppose, Minnie, that you managed to find the only cowboy in Texas who paints faces?"

"At this rodeo, Momma," Minnie said. "At least I didn't see any others. And even if I did, I'd still want Calhoun to do it, 'cause he's an awesome painter. He can paint a pretty naked woman, Momma," she added as Calhoun gently wiped off the blue splash of paint he'd put on Olivia's cheek.

Olivia looked behind her at the exhibits where people were milling around, gazing at the paintings. "I...see."

"Ah, Minnie," Calhoun said, taking her face in his hands to finish her unicorn. "You certainly are mini," he told her. "But I suspect you're high voltage all the time." Then he painted a sparkly unicorn on her cheek.

Kenny scooted a barrel next to Calhoun so he

could intently watch the process now that he had a deer on his cheek. Olivia hung back, her boot tapping nervously on the ground.

"These customers waited patiently for their turns," Calhoun said conversationally to Olivia, hoping to calm her down. They were all breaking the rules, and he suspected she wasn't buying the paying customer routine, but he knew the kids were after a little attention. He was willing to supply it until everybody said *sayonara* tomorrow night, so what was the harm? As their mother said, they pestered *everybody* for attention.

And Minnie wanted him to paint a doctored-up portrait of her and her brother that represented the image in her mind, the one she wished for. An image that was right up there with the idea of unicorns being the fabled symbol of happiness.

He couldn't give the kids what they wanted, any more than he could give them real unicorns. Or an idealized family with picture-perfect hair and dolled-up dresses.

He knew all about trying to create a reality out of the painted picture in one's mind of the perfect family. "There," he said gently to Minnie. "The best one I've done all day." And he rumpled Kenny's hair so that the spit-combing was shot. "Yours, too, kid. Y'all got the best I had."

"Thanks, Mr. Calhoun," Kenny said. Getting up, he went to his mom so she could inspect the artwork. "You should let him paint your face, Mom," he said.

"It feels kinda funny when he touches you, but you'd like it."

Olivia blushed deeply. She could feel it, because it felt as if she'd just broken out in some kind of flu-like rash. Glancing at Calhoun, she was grateful to see that he was pretending not to hear. He was, simply, the most beautiful, clean-shaven and sexy-smelling cowboy she'd ever met, and her heart thump-thump-thumped in warning. She knew all about how wonderful it felt when he touched her face.

She laid a ten on the table to pay for the face painting. "Thank you. Kids, let's go."

"Thank you," they told Calhoun, and then hugged his neck, being careful not to smudge their painted faces.

"You're welcome," he said, not looking at Olivia or the ten dollars. "Goodbye."

Olivia didn't know what to do except stiffly walk away, her gaze anywhere but on the paintings.

The worst part was, he *did* paint extraordinary nudes.

Chapter Four

After putting the kids to bed that evening, Olivia decided to sit out on the stoop of their motor home. The evening air was inviting, and she wasn't ready to crawl in bed. She needed to think, and the topic of her thoughts was Calhoun. The paint had now faded some from the children's faces—they wouldn't remove the art at bedtime, claiming the drawings were special—but her thoughts about Calhoun were in no danger of fading at all. She felt as though her heart was running away inside her chest, wild and free where she couldn't lasso it or tell it to calm down.

"I'm too old for such silliness," she murmured, scratching at a bug bite on her leg just below her shorts.

"Ms. Spinlove," she heard Calhoun say. "You forgot this." He held out the ten dollars she'd left for him.

Her heart raced faster, thrilled to be out of reach of the lasso. "We're paying customers."

"I'll charge you when I've actually worked for it. Your kids are a pleasure."

Of course he would say that, the louse. A man who painted women's naked bodies as brilliantly as he did also knew their minds intimately, no doubt. Everything was laid bare before him. "Please don't sweet-talk me. I'm real sensitive about my kids."

"You should be. May I?"

He asked permission to sit next to her on the stoop. She didn't want him to, but there was no place else to sit, and besides, it seemed somewhat rude after he'd put the money back in his pocket to save her pride. It wasn't as if he was going to kiss her again— though her feminine wishes delighted at the thought.

"I didn't just come to return the money," Calhoun said. "I also wanted to tell you that we didn't deliberately go against your rules today. I kind of got caught in the cross fire. Your daughter watched me paint a little girl's face, and—" he shot her a glance she'd have to call pleading "—Olivia, I couldn't send Minnie away. The hope for a face tattoo was written all over her. And Kenny looked so old and wise and sad—"

"I told you," she interrupted. "They're worriers. And it shows. So people worry about them." She sighed deeply. "I don't know why they worry as much as they do."

"Probably because they see you doing it. And you talk to them like they're little adults. Which is not an entirely bad thing, but it does make them realize that the world around them requires some figuring out rather than magical zippedee-do-da."

"You're right," she said, surprised.

"Of course I am." He leaned back against the stoop to rest on his elbows. "I recognize them. They are like me. Our souls are the same."

She laughed. "What are you talking about?"

"Trust me. I know all about childhood worries." He picked a blade of grass that was growing stubbornly in the gravel-and-dirt drive. "It won't kill them to know that the world is a serious place. They're just skipping over those later years when a lot of kids experience dislocated reality."

"Are you sure?"

"Yeah. I turned out fine, didn't I?"

"I don't know," she said slowly. "You paint gorgeous naked women. On the one hand, I admire it, and on the other hand, it scares me."

He smiled. "I sold about six of those paintings today, and I definitely made enough money to buy you a beer. How about it?"

Instantly, she shook her head. "No, thanks, but congratulations, just the same. Does that include the naked saddle Minnie was so fascinated by?"

She was amazed to see Calhoun look uncomfortable.

"You know, that was a wholly inappropriate remark Minnie and Kenny shouldn't have heard. I'm sorry about that, Olivia. I didn't know the old coot was going to say what he did, and I didn't realize your kids were hiding out behind the easels."

"They hear plenty in the rodeo and they know

how to handle it. I'm not worried about them. So, was the saddle an extra sale?"

He blew out a breath. "Yes. And she's supposed to look like Marilyn Monroe." His expression was sheepish. "I'm sort of known for painting breasts."

She didn't know what to say to that, but at the same time, she was pretty proud of her B cups. Okay, so they weren't grandiose, but she filled out her rodeo blouses just fine.

"Big or small, it doesn't matter to me," Calhoun said, waving his hand to show he didn't have a preference. "It's the shading and shape, the slope of the breast, that draws my artistic passion."

"I assume you just like women a lot—and have known quite a variety of them, judging by your work." She looked at him straight on. "My guess is that you're something of a womanizer."

"Absolutely not," he said. "Although, I do like the companionship of women. At my ranch, women are quite the…uh, topic of reverence. We really respect 'em."

"Really?" She wondered if he was telling the truth or trying to impress her. "You had sisters?"

"Um, no."

"Ah. Your mother taught you to respect women."

"Not exactly. I mean, she would have, but she wasn't around long enough to complete the lessons in our teen years. We had Mimi," Calhoun said, frowning. "Our next-door neighbor, but she was such a hellion growing up we thought she was one of us until she sprouted breasts. Sheriff, her father, made her quit swimming with us without her shirt on. I can't tell you how mad she was that she could no longer swim in her jean cutoffs like we did.

"I can't say Mimi taught us to respect women, because we treated her like a brother." He scratched his head under his hat.

"Poor Mimi," Olivia said, "whoever she is."

"So," Calhoun said brightly, "we learned to appreciate women ourselves."

"Ourselves?"

"Me and my eleven brothers."

Olivia hesitated. "You live, basically, in a huge bachelor pad of twelve males. No discipline. No female presence to provide sanity."

"Maybe that's why I like breasts so much," Calhoun said thoughtfully. "We had bare, flat chests, lots of testosterone and no female influence. Except Mimi, and she doesn't count because—"

"She was one of you. Until she changed. I got it."

"Actually, she was still one of us, even then. We just felt sorry for her because she had to wear a shirt over her cutoffs."

"Couldn't she wear a bathing suit?"

Calhoun turned to stare at her. "Oh, no, we would really have freaked out if she'd looked *that* different from us. Mimi was like our brother, the thirteenth man, the thinker of the group, if you will. Sheriff let her run wild as a March hare, and we got into all our best trouble when Mimi was around."

Olivia sighed. "So, back to the bachelor pad with twelve males. I guess there's plenty of *Playboy* magazines lying around."

He snapped his fingers. "That's how I learned I loved breasts!"

She gave him a wry look. "Calhoun, you're a different breed than I've met before."

"But so harmless," he said. "I am probably the easiest, most harmless man you'll ever meet."

She was about to express some doubt on that when a motorcycle pulled up in front of them. When the rider took off his helmet, a Mohawk was revealed, as well as a jet-black cross earring that made a statement that was anything but religious. And he wore decorated, expensive boots to make a man proud.

"Hey, Calhoun."

Calhoun shot to his feet. "Last! What are you doing here? And on this motorcycle?"

"She's all mine," Last said, "and I'm in love. She's got all the right moves, and she's built to please."

Calhoun started to inspect the motorcycle, then straightened. "Last, this is Olivia Spinlove. Olivia, the youngest of the Jefferson tribe, Last. How'd you find me?"

"I asked some cowboys. They said you'd probably be here. Sparking."

"I am not sparking," Calhoun said with an embarrassed glance at Olivia. "We're just having a friendly chat."

"Cool. All right. I just dropped by to say hello before I leave town."

"Wait." Calhoun glanced at Olivia, a quick check to see if she was listening, which she was—with interest. "Leave town?"

"Yeah." Last grinned. "I got a haircut so my head won't get hot under a helmet, bought me a baby of a bike, and now I'm off to see the country. Which I've never done much of before. I need to get out of town bad."

"Hang on a minute. This means you haven't told Mason yet about…" He sent a furtive glance Olivia's way.

"I'll tell him when I get back," Last said.

"Last." Calhoun sighed, taking a moment to formulate his thoughts. "I think you should head on back and tell Mason the truth. To his face, because you know he's going to find out in your absence. Avoiding the conversation may be tempting, but I vote for the up-front approach. And, you know he hates motorcycles. For him, it's trucks only. Anything with two wheels is basically a vanity item, and the ranch doesn't need the expense of vanity." He gave his brother a narrow stare. "What I'm basically saying here, bro, is that you're going down the path of disaster, where Mason is concerned, but there's still time to turn back."

Last shook his head. "Calhoun, you don't understand. If you were in my boots, you'd know that my life's about useless right now, anyway."

"That doesn't mean you should ride off and leave your responsibilities behind. That won't up your useful quotient."

Last's eyes turned hard. "Man, you have no idea how tough it is knowing that Valentine's on the ranch every day. I never know when I might see her, and I don't want to. So I live daily running away from my mistake. We get along fine, and when the baby arrives this month, I'm sure I'll love it. But Navarro should never have brought her to the ranch. Nobody was thinking about how I might feel about it. The part that really pisses me off is that you all had your wild nights, and days, and women you never saw again. But me," Last said bitterly, "I had a night I barely remember and an endless hangover—fatherhood." He put his helmet back on. "Sure, I wanted kids around the ranch. I wanted some of my brothers to start families. But *I* didn't want to be a father."

Calhoun heard a door close behind him. Olivia had retreated. He couldn't blame her. "I thought you got past the weird phase with the funky hair and the earring. The binge drinking."

"I'm not drinking. I'm just going to see the world while I still can," Last said, his voice determined.

Calhoun sighed. "Do what you have to do, I guess. Did you even tell anyone you were leaving?"

"I told *you.*" Last revved the motorcycle. "It seemed fitting, since you were in Lonely Hearts Station, where my sin was born. But you know," Last said, his tone angry now, "you'll have your fun here and it will stay here. It won't come to live with you at the ranch, staring you in the face. You'll love it and leave it, and your sin will be the cost of a condom. Cheapest fun on the planet."

He saluted Calhoun sardonically with two fingers and rode away. Calhoun stared after his youngest brother, his heart sad for the family philosopher. So much had changed. Gone were the rose-colored glasses they'd always teased their youngest brother about—Calhoun felt as if his own innocence had slipped away, as well.

He turned to stare at the trailer door that Olivia had escaped through. *Gone like the wind,* one might say, if one was in the mood to utilize titles from bygone eras to describe a relationship that was obviously never going to be. Shaking his head, he strode away.

He couldn't blame Olivia Spinlove for not wanting any part of him or Malfunction Junction. She had enough malfunction on her hands, and truthfully, he admired her for shutting the door on the possibility of more.

BARLEY SPINLOVE waited until he was certain his daughter was through listening at the window. He watched her disappear down the hall and heard her get into bed with her children.

All right. So wearing clown makeup wasn't the way he wanted to have this conversation, but he didn't have the reputation of meanness for nothing. A man had to protect his family. And Calhoun Jefferson was trouble. The Jeffersons were infamous in the rodeo world. Their reputations stretched for miles and stank like unwashed hounds. He hadn't minded a bit of conversation between Calhoun and Olivia— she could take care of herself.

But his tiny window had been open at his end of the motor home—and he, too, had heard every word of the Jefferson conversation. Best he put in a few words of his own.

Quietly, he opened the door and headed after the departing cowboy. "You," he said.

Calhoun turned around.

Barley came to a stop in front of him, a good foot shorter in stature, but making up for it with attitude. "I want you to shove off. Olivia doesn't need you hanging around. Nothing good can come from a Jefferson wolf hanging around my lamb."

Calhoun stared at the robust, frowning clown in front of him. "I mean Olivia no harm."

"I'm not interested in your sales shtick. I know who you are, and I know where you'll end up, in a darkened corner somewhere or a cheap hotel with my daughter, sweet-talking her into believing you're different from your brothers. Olivia's got good sense, and I'm sure she recognizes by now that the Jefferson men are light on commitment and long on baloney, but her heart's been busted before. It ain't gonna happen again. And especially not to those kids. As I oughta know, sparkly face paint wears off, cowboy. You can quit wooing those kids to get to their mother.

It just ain't gonna happen while I'm alive." He gave Calhoun a belligerent stare.

Calhoun shook his head. "That's not the way I meant it."

"It don't matter," Barley said. "I say shove off, I mean shove off, and it'd be best if you recalled that."

The clown walked away. Calhoun scratched his head, watching the man's angry, stiff stride. He could certainly understand Barley's protective stance, and he could see where he got his reputation.

"On the other hand," Calhoun murmured, "I've never been told to shove off before."

Generally, fathers were happy to have the Jeffersons come a'courtin', as they called it. The Jeffersons had a reputation for being wild, but they also had a huge ranch. A lot of money. A rep for playing hard, working hard. No one had ever thrown them out of anywhere, except maybe from a bar or two when the owner thought the brothers as a whole were too rowdy.

But they'd never been told not to come back. Just come back when y'all are more fitting. Jefferson money and Jefferson manpower were usually pretty damn welcome.

Shove off wasn't sitting too well in Calhoun's gut.

He stared at the trailer a few more minutes.

He liked Minnie and Kenny, and truth be told, he hadn't tried to romance them. They'd romanced *him*, if the story were repeated without bias.

He didn't figure Barley cared too much for anyone's bias but his own.

Calhoun slowly smiled, years of Jefferson determination and grit flowing through him. *Shove off* was practically an engraved invitation: *Romance my daughter, please. RSVP in the affirmative.*

I'm beggin' ya.

Chapter Five

Olivia had heard every word of the conversation between Last and Calhoun. It scared her. If anything could have shown her that she was in the company of a rogue, Calhoun's brother showing up was just the thing to splash cold water on her newborn daydreams. Calhoun would not be a good thing for her nor for her children, and as she sat on the bed watching Minnie and Kenny sleep, Olivia knew she couldn't see him anymore.

No matter how wonderful a kisser he was. Even if he opened up a vista of longing she'd never experienced before. Simply put, Calhoun was a nightmare, not a dream man.

Kenny stirred, his little hand touching the painted mark on his face. Her kids were drawn to men, to the cowboys they knew from growing up in the rodeo circuit. They were innocent, much like Mimi had been running around without her shirt on, bathing in the swimming hole with the Jefferson boys. She'd been the mischief queen of her merry band of misfits because it was all she'd ever known.

Growing up in the company of men was harmless now, Olivia decided, seeing the parallel between Mimi's experience and that of her own children. But later, it might not be harmless. They would end up like Olivia, abandoned by the men they'd trusted without the useful and supportive role of female friends in their lives. You couldn't understand a woman's world unless you'd been around other women. Mothers, sisters, aunts, friends.

Olivia's eyes widened. She made a decision.

A woman who didn't like to be intimate could never expect to keep a man, especially not a macho man like Calhoun. The feeling of scratchy faces, bungling hands and sometimes smelly bodies just wasn't Olivia's cup of tea. Oh, the other gals in the rodeo ran after cowboys like they were sweet icing on a cake—but what did they know? They wanted a man.

She didn't. She'd had one. And though her family had come to her at great cost, they were more than she'd ever expected out of life. Though her father adored the trophies they won and the show business career, Olivia knew that was all glitter and glue. Her *kids* were her dreams realized.

A tapping on her window surprised her. Leaning over Minnie and Kenny, she opened the motor home window. "What are you doing?" she demanded of Calhoun.

"Hoping you'll give me a chance to explain."

"Explain what?"

Calhoun grimaced. "About my brother."

"You don't owe me an explanation."

"I do if I ever want to see you again," he said. "I can tell you got spooked."

She stared at him through the screen. "Why would you ever want to see me again? Not that we're seeing each other."

"Of course we're not," Calhoun said, "not through that damn screen anyway. Come out."

"I will not."

"Olivia, we're going to wake the children."

"No, we're not, because this conversation is over." She started to close the window.

"Don't go," he said, and she hesitated. "I swear you should ease up on me. I'm not the bad man you think I am."

Well, he wasn't a bad man, per se, except maybe for her. Her heart gleefully outwitted the lasso trying to constrain it. "You're not a bad man. But you're probably not a good man, either."

"Well, women don't like good men. Good men finish last, I always say," Calhoun said. "Although there are varying degrees of good and bad. You want a man with a little toughness to him, or else you might as well be living with a woman."

"Precisely what I was thinking," Olivia said. "I should be learning about life from women."

Calhoun blinked. "You liked kissing me, Olivia. I know you're afraid of me, but I am not that scary.

Come out here and let me kiss you again, and I'll prove it."

She shook her head. "That's not what I need. I might look Marvella up. I might quit the rodeo and stay here. Maybe it's time for our act to come to an end."

Calhoun drew closer to the screen. "Marvella is not the woman you want to bond with."

"My father liked her well enough," Olivia said.

"Well, your father isn't…never mind," Calhoun said. "If you come out, I'll teach you about the stars."

She was oh so tempted.

"And if you don't want to learn about the stars, I can teach you about something else. Anything your heart desires to know," he said, his voice husky.

"Go, Momma," Minnie said, her eyes open wide and looking up at her.

"Shh," Olivia said. "Go back to sleep, angel."

"I can't. You woke me up with all that whispering. Adults never realize that a child's ears listen for whispers. We wouldn't listen if you were talking in normal voices, but when you and Grandpa are whispering, me and Kenny know we better be paying attention."

Olivia smiled at her daughter. "You can be an angel, but you have your rascal side, too."

Minnie rolled over, closed her eyes and tucked her hands under her chin. "I come by it honestly, Grandpa says. Go see Calhoun, Momma. He's not the three-headed rattler you told us the bounty bull was. He's not mean."

"True." Olivia shook her head. She had an example to set for her children, and whispering through a window to a cowboy wasn't the one she should be setting. "Good night, Calhoun," she said, closing the window.

She tried not to notice his disappointment.

"Momma," Minnie said ruefully, rolling back over to look at her. "Why don't you like him?"

"Oh, sweetie." Olivia brushed her daughter's long hair away from her face. "Did you brush your hair today?"

"If I answer honestly, will you answer honestly?" Minnie asked.

Olivia laughed, kissed her daughter's forehead and rose from the bed. "No. Now good night."

Minnie rolled back and closed her eyes. "Good night, Momma."

Olivia turned on the small night-light, overrode the urge to peek out and see if Calhoun was still hanging around and then told herself it didn't matter.

He'd convinced her that now was not the time for her to dream of settling in one place. Especially not within reach of his easy appeal. Calhoun and his painted women.

Everything inside her was telling her to run this time.

CALHOUN STRODE AWAY from the motor home, wishing Last was around so he could kick him. Everything had been going along just fine, until his boneheaded brother showed up! All Olivia had needed was an excuse to steer clear of him, and crazy-looking, stubborn Last had given her excuses aplenty.

He might never get his lips locked to hers again. Calhoun found that a depressing thought.

His cell phone rang. "Hello?" he asked.

"Hey," Archer said. "Last been your way?"

"Yeah," Calhoun said. "The big plan spoiler."

"What?"

"Never mind. What's up?" Calhoun asked, resigned to the occasional hell that his brothers could be.

"Tell Last to get his ass home," Archer said. "Mason's in full froth that he just up and left like that."

"No can do. Boy Wonder is long gone on his Wonderbike."

"Meaning?"

"He rode out of town on an expensive motorcycle. Was wearing boots that cost a buck's antlers, and he's slipped back into goth mode. Attack of Mohawk Man. Earring, too. If I was a betting man, I'd be betting a tattoo parlor was his next stop. But he says he's not drinking, so I'm trying to be grateful for something."

Silence met his words.

"Okay," Archer finally said. "Did he give you a timetable for his return?"

"Nope. Said he had to get away from his life, or some drama like that."

"Damn it! Mason's gonna crap."

Calhoun nodded in sympathy as he ambled into a bar, claiming a bar stool for his own. The bar keeper came over and Calhoun pointed to the hanging sign advertising a beer. A second later, a beer sat in front of him: yellow genie in a bottle. "If only it were so easy," he murmured.

"What?" Archer asked.

"Never mind." He took a huge swig. "So, tell Mason he's gonna be shorthanded awhile, I guess."

"When are you coming back? Did you ride the bull?"

"Ride would be too optimistic a verb," Calhoun said. "I would choose *cling*. Did I cling, you ask? No, I clung perhaps three seconds, and then lost my pride somewhere south of Bloodthirsty's hooves. However, two sweet children saw my shame and came to cheer me up."

"Last thing I'd want around is rug rats after I'd been thrown," Archer said dryly. "So, are you coming back?"

"Not tonight. I'm nursing my pride. Because not only did I get thrown, but I got thrown, if you get my drift. Right off my game."

"Ah. Woman-quest. Good for you. I was worried about you when you said sweet children had comforted you in your moment of shame. Glad to know you're at least allowing women to speak to you. You've been very prickly about the female species lately. We were all starting to wonder."

"She's the mother of the two children I mentioned," Calhoun said on a growl.

"Oh," Archer said. "Good play."

"I did not play them. They played me." Calhoun was getting very ruffled with his brother, and even the yellow genie in a bottle wasn't helping him relax.

"How's the art? Still full breasted?"

Calhoun blinked. Olivia wasn't what he'd call full breasted. Breasts weren't what made a woman beautiful anyway, but he didn't expect his brothers to understand his particular appreciation of the female form. When he transferred his visions to canvas, they merely saw breasts. Which was strange, considering the women were completely naked, he mused. Of course, maybe the breasts he painted drew the eye more since he spent so much time laboring over them.

God, he loved breasts, and he had a pretty good notion Olivia's would suit his artistic desires very well, though a man would have a devil of a time getting that woman's bra off. He had a better shot at putting a bra on Bloodthirsty. He frowned. How in the hell would he get Olivia's bra off? An erection grew inside his jeans and he shifted, feeling ornery.

"I might never see the one pair of nipples I believe I was destined to view," he muttered.

"Hello?" Archer said. "Are we having the same conversation? Because I'm pretty certain I wasn't participating. Although if we're talking real life and not still life, I might want to get in on it."

"You couldn't handle this crew, trust me."

Archer laughed. "All right. Listen, you're going to have to cut your quest short. Mason's mood is worse than ever, and when I tell him Last has hit the trail, he's really going to flip. I don't want to be the one to give him the worst news. You're going to have to be here for the family caucus."

Calhoun frowned. "The caucus to tell him that Last has pulled a 'Mason' and run off? I think Mason should recognize that his own reaction to disenfranchisement was the same as Last's and suck it up. That is to say, he hit the trail first, wearing his tail tight between his back legs. Last's just following family tradition. And God, we have a lot of family tradition."

"No," Archer said. "I meant the caucus to tell him that Mimi's selling her ranch."

"What?" Calhoun sat up straight, tightening his grip on the beer bottle.

"That's right. Selling out. Gettin' out while the gettin's good. Or as good as it's gonna get anyway."

"Why?" Life as they'd known it and revered it seemed to suddenly be grinding to a halt. Maybe it had been skidding for a long time, and they'd all simply ignored it, hoping the skid would stop.

"The short answer is, she can't take care of her property and her sick dad and her baby. Even with the housekeeper helping out. Long answer? That's a mighty big place for one little lady to manage, and if any of us thought Mimi's soon-to-be ex-husband was going to be a ranch man, we were destined to be disappointed. He's a city-slick lawyer, not a cowboy. Not that I'm criticizing…"

"But you are criticizing," Calhoun said. "Because Brian never did come home to Mimi."

"I'm merely saying their marriage arrangement didn't include him living here. And obviously, it didn't include her living in Austin or Houston." He sighed. "The final nail was probably Mason's long trip since he'd been doing most of the work over there after the sheriff took sick. But Mason was gone too long, and Mimi got overwhelmed, I guess. She's decided to tell everybody in town officially that her father can't resume his duties, and she's taking them over. She figures she can do a better job of sheriffing and everything else she's got to manage from town."

"Yeah, I'm hearing that," Calhoun said slowly, "but it sure is hard to swallow." He felt terribly guilty. Sure, they'd all tried to pick up a little slack at Mimi's place, but with the brothers marrying one by one and heading off with their new brides, Mason's absence and Last's paternity lawsuit, they'd been shorthanded.

He ground his teeth. "I should pack up and come home tonight."

"Well, normally I would say hell, yeah. But it's been a long time since I've heard you mention a flesh-and-blood woman, Calhoun. And you ain't talking about painting her, either."

"I painted her kids' faces," Calhoun said gruffly. "I'd like to do a portrait of them. They're pretty cute for rodeo brats."

"And so," Archer said, "maybe you should ease out of there slowly tomorrow. No point in running home. I'm in no hurry to face Mason with Mimi's news."

"Don't suppose she'd tell him herself."

"Even if she did, she'd still want us around for moral support. You know, something's not quite right with our Mimi."

Calhoun swigged from his bottle and waved for another, though at this point, he knew the yellow genie of relaxation was not going to have her way with his tension tonight. "Do you have anything more on that hunch?"

"No. It's just feels like something's not right."

"You felt this while she was unburdening her plans to you?"

"Yeah. It was the strangest thing," Archer said. "I could tell she really didn't want to talk to Mason. You don't think she's mad at him for being gone so long, do you?"

Who knew what went on in a woman's brain? They had emotions all over them, even etched into their eyelids, so delicate that a man could pierce their feelings without even meaning to. Calhoun closed his eyes, thinking about Olivia. Olivia was one big emotion. Not in a bad way, of course. But he could tell he'd have to tread carefully with her for a long time, if he had a long time—which he didn't—and if he was of a mind to romance her.

Which he wasn't. Romance wasn't his thing.

Seduction, then.

No. Even Jefferson males on their horniest days didn't seduce emotionally tender females.

"Crap," he muttered. "This is all going from bad to worse."

"I know. I feel like a clothesline that got caught in a storm. Whipped and tangled."

Calhoun shook his head. "I'll be home tomorrow night. We'll kick it around a bit more before we tell Mason." Sighing, he turned off the phone, putting it back into his pocket. "Oh, Mason's not going to take that well," he said aloud. "Jefferson men seem to have endless woman trouble. It should be so easy for us. We clean up good, we're strong, we're smart…"

He slumped a little, trying to absorb what Archer had told him. This was simply not going to be good. He was sure matters had taken a flashing-red-light turn for the worse.

Someone lightly tapped him on the shoulder. He turned.

Olivia stood beside him, her eyes wide, her lips trembling, obviously wrestling with her thoughts and trying hard to be brave.

And then she wrapped her arms around his neck and kissed him.

Chapter Six

Olivia caught him so off guard that Calhoun didn't have a chance to hesitate, nor wonder why he was getting such a gift. By the time she'd put her lips so sweetly against his, two or three times, he gave over to base instinct and pulled her into his lap. The empty beer bottle went spinning away but he held fast to Olivia, drinking her in as fast as a man could gulp when offered such nectar.

If he was a gentleman, he'd have understood she wouldn't have searched him out in a bar if something wasn't troubling her. But he was just a man, though smart enough to give her everything she wanted.

Besides, she felt way too good. He wouldn't stop to ask questions. They could talk later.

The bar erupted in cheers and hoots and catcalls. Calhoun didn't want to let her go, but Olivia seemed to regain her former stiffness. Breaking away, she stared at him, her eyes large, her mouth rosy and a little swollen from the heat with which he'd kissed her.

Ah, if she'd only let him kiss her some more, he

could really send her away looking like a well-kissed woman.

With a guilty glance around the bar, Olivia turned and hurried off. He watched her sweetly fitting jeans go with regret. A woman whose backside filled out Wrangler jeans the way hers did ought to be on canvas.

"You Jefferson dawgs have all the luck," someone called. "Women just throw themselves at you."

"Shut up," he called back good-naturedly. Olivia hadn't thrown herself at him, because if she had, he'd have caught her for certain. She'd merely been testing herself.

If he hurried, maybe he could catch her while she was still in test mode.

Tossing some money on the bar, he ran after Olivia.

"Go, Calhoun, go!" someone cried out to a burst of rowdy cheers.

He ignored the applause and caught up to Olivia. "Hey," he said, catching her hand to turn her to him. In the faint light from the tents, he could see her eyes, big and serious, as she looked up at him. "What was that for?"

She cocked her head. "Earlier you said I was afraid."

"Yeah? So?"

He watched her take a deep breath. "I'm not afraid. Not as much as you are." Removing her hand from his, she strode away.

Tricky little minx. He'd have his way with her on

some level, just to satisfy his curiosity. "No fair, cowgirl," he said, catching up to her so he could grab her hand more securely this time and turn her toward his chest. "It's only verbal foreplay when you toss out dares and then run off. You know I have to catch you and participate, or we'll never move to second base, which is verbal seduction."

She stared at him. "Verbal seduction?"

"Ah, yes. The thinking part, if you will, of the chase. Listen and learn." He pulled her underneath a light-strung tree, slowly kissed each of her palms in turn, then put his lips against her ear. "You're beautiful," he said, and when she would have moved away, in doubt, he held her delicate chin against him so that his lips touched her ear while he caressed her neck with his fingers.

"You are beautiful in so many ways you can't even understand, because it takes an outsider to see the whole you. And maybe it takes an artistic eye to see what you can never see. You're fun. You're tricky. You hold all your hopes and dreams and worries in your sexy eyes, and men would give the use of their roping arms to lie with you at night. You're hot, Olivia Spinlove. Where you see Mother when you look in the mirror, men see Catch Me If You Can. And we want to so bad."

She was standing still. His words had completely stunned her. Now, he would tell her exactly what only the wild part of her sheltered little heart dreamed of knowing.

"You rock a man with your body and your tease, Olivia, and because you don't do it deliberately, you come off sweet. So sweet that a man can taste you just by looking at you. It makes him dream of having you melt on his tongue."

"Stop," she said, backing up slightly.

He let her move away, watching her like a hawk.

She hesitated, her eyes so wide he knew he would live with that memory forever.

Then she turned and fled.

He snorted to himself, watching her go with satisfaction, his nostrils flared, his jeans full of unspent heat. "*Now* who's scared?" he said to her perfume as it lingered gently on the nighttime wind.

OLIVIA QUIETLY let herself into the motor home, careful not to wake her family. She was burning from Calhoun's words—and the shocking part was that he'd never kissed her after he'd caught her. He'd merely used words to ravish her.

Words the woman in her had thrilled to hear.

She sank onto the bed next to her children, surprised to find herself trembling a little. Passion was not a well-met friend. It was, if anything, a passing acquaintance that had often left her stranded.

But tonight her heart raced and her breath seemed tight, and she wanted to run back to Calhoun and beg him to say everything he'd said again so that she could remember it, and please, would he mean it, damn it, because she so badly wanted to be the woman he claimed he saw—

"Pathetic," she whispered to herself.

Kenny murmured in his sleep. Olivia glanced over at him, then gasped as she looked at her two beautiful sleeping children.

She was falling! After warning herself over and over again about falling for a man, especially a charming cowboy who clearly knew his way around lots of women, she had practically begged him to seduce her! She was to blame for going after him and taunting him—and he was right. It was verbal foreplay she'd been offering, a path that could only end in her own disaster. Again. Hadn't she burdened her father—her family—enough?

The Jeffersons were not settling types, as evidenced by Calhoun's younger brother Last, who rebelliously escaped his responsibilities. And Calhoun, painter of naked women, what would make him settle for just one? If Olivia ever fell for another man again, it would have to be someone serious, who would love Kenny and Minnie as much as a man could, in the role of father.

Calhoun couldn't.

And there she was, practically begging him to make love to her.

In fact, her body had told him everything he'd needed to know. She was his for the taking.

It was only the gentleman in him that had kept him from doing more than whispering seduction in her ear.

Olivia turned off the tiny night-light and curled up next to her children.

From now on, she would watch herself closely. Thank God she'd realized the disastrous path she was on.

BY MORNING, CALHOUN had a hangover but it wasn't from the yellow genie. It was from sitting up all night thinking about the little barrel rider and her family. What was it about her that made him want to possess her so badly? Did he see himself in her and her dis-organized gypsy band of a family?

Heaven knew the Jeffersons were gypsylike. Whether it was the attics of their minds, the lay of the land or the hearts of women, the Jefferson men wandered.

By God, Olivia made him want to make a pit stop.

She was dangerous to his way of life. Or perhaps, his lack of a way of life. He had no way. He had the ranch and a load of paintings. He had artistic vision.

He had a half-baked erection he couldn't shake no matter how much he thought about cold things.

Maybe a long swim in Barmaid's Creek was what he needed. December's chill on the water oughta knock the stiffness out of his drill.

And it would clear his head. Keep him away from those treacherous children of Olivia's. They were a huge part of the problem. They wanted him. They'd said so, and he could feel it, and it made him want them, too.

"How dumb is that, huh?" he muttered, pulling on his plain, worn-down brown riding boots. "What you need, Calhoun, is to bring a few more children into this family for a while, because we don't have enough men acting like kids. Yes, we need more responsibilities, because we're managing so well with the ones we've got."

No wonder Mimi was selling her ranch. It wasn't as if they'd exactly helped out their little neighbor in need. They'd tried, but Mimi needed a full-time man.

And so did Olivia.

"The Jefferson track record does suck," he told a small cricket in the windowsill. He finished packing and left money on the bed for Delilah—she wouldn't take it if he tried to give it to her in person. She'd given all the Jeffersons a key to the back door of her salon so they could go up the back stairs and stay whenever they were in town. A phone call was all she required, so she could make them breakfast.

A favor given was a favor returned, Delilah Honeycutt said. Since the big storm had brought Delilah and her crew of Lonely Hearts Station stylists to the ranch, there'd been plenty of favors between them.

"Goodbye little cricket. I'm going to do *you* a favor and put you outside where you can find a girlfriend," he said. "Because all you're going to find in this windowsill is smashed. And hey, I figure you, as an ugly critter only suited for swimming on the end of a fishing hook, have even less chance of getting love all figured out before you meet your cricket end than I do."

He carried his duffel and the cricket to his truck. The duffel he tossed into the truck bed; the cricket he laid carefully in the grass. "Jump on," he told it. "I'm going to go jump on some eggs and bacon."

Somewhere far from Olivia's motor home. After this afternoon's exhibit of his paintings, he was going to pack up and return to Malfunction Junction.

Where he belonged. His own little patch of grass.

"DO YOU THINK Calhoun will come to see our act?" Minnie asked her mother as Olivia finished putting makeup on her dad's face.

It seemed to Olivia that Barley bristled under her fingertips. "Unsquinch your face, Dad," she said. "The white will crack if you keep doing that.

"No," she said to the children who eagerly anticipated her answer. "No, I don't think Calhoun will come. He has to go back home sometime, and we have to hit the road. Tonight's the last night."

Minnie's face seemed shadowed. Kenny's eyes dimmed a bit as he glanced at his grandfather. "How are your knees?" Kenny asked. "Are you feeling good?"

"I'm feeling fine, Kenny." Barley ruffled his grandson's hair affectionately. "Don't you worry about me. I've got more jump in me than a cricket."

Kenny blinked. "I love you, Grandpa."

Barley nodded, and despite the clown makeup drawn around his eyes, Olivia could see the glimmer of unshed emotion.

"Hey," Barley told him. "I've got a surprise for you tonight."

"You do?" Kenny and Minnie asked hopefully.

"I do," Barley said. His eyes met Olivia's in the mirror.

Olivia tried to smile, but she couldn't. Her heart was too heavy. The well of sadness was too darkly puzzling. Why should she care if she never saw Calhoun again?

The smile slipped from her father's face. Olivia blinked as she realized Barley had read her emotions.

"Damn it, Olivia," he said.

She burst into tears and fled to the back of the motor home.

BUT AN HOUR LATER, Olivia was in full control of herself. She wore her riding costume, a rhinestone-sparkled pair of jeans, a silky white tie top and white boots with fringes. Her expression felt as painted on as her father's.

"I'm ready," she told him, raising her chin.

He looked at her for a minute, then nodded. "I'm sorry," he said.

"There's no reason to ever be sorry in a family," she told him. "You're right. And I'm fine."

"Still." He reached out and softly touched her hair. "I shouldn't have spoken to you that way."

"It's all right."

They looked at each other another moment, and then she walked out the door to saddle Gypsy. The kids silently helped her, while Barley closed up the motor home. Olivia's stiff movements felt unnatural to her. She caught herself glancing over her shoulder toward the open pathway, and then realized she was looking for Calhoun.

After that, she turned her back and kept her gaze solely on the task at hand.

She had never been so glad to be leaving a place in all her riding career. Lonely Hearts Station, indeed. Her father had his feelings hurt by a woman who lived here, and now she had bad memories of her own to pack up and take with her.

She hoped Calhoun was gone by now. She hadn't left the trailer all day. She hadn't wanted to run into him before his exhibit was finished. The kids had played Yahtzee with her, and cards, and they'd baked chocolate chip cookies that they'd cut from a roll. It had been a sweet interlude, just the four of them, resting together as a family until show time.

And now it was show time.

Time to show herself that she wasn't the same girl who'd fallen for the last cowboy who'd pretended to give her his heart.

Thirty minutes later, she had Gypsy in the breezeway of the arena. It was packed tonight, which was good, because Gypsy loved crowds. She seemed to perform best when she had a big arena.

Barley agreed with Olivia on that. He said Gypsy was a true show horse, born to love the limelight.

"Well, you are an ole lime," Olivia told the horse

affectionately, rubbing under the horse's mane. "And look at all that light you get tonight."

She held back the curtain, telling herself she wasn't scanning the crowd for Calhoun. Why would he be here, anyway? That cowboy with his flowery and earnest words was long gone.

Verbal foreplay. She petted the horse's neck. "All I wanted was to know that I wasn't afraid, you know. That's not wrong, Gypsy. And you know what? With the right man, I might have been a good wife."

Gypsy tossed her head.

"Oo-la-la," Olivia said. "Aren't we the fiery miss tonight?"

She swung up into the saddle, as Kenny and Minnie waited by the curtain.

"Good luck, Momma," Minnie called.

"Good luck, Gypsy," Kenny said.

Olivia rode into the ring, her heart nearly stopping as she realized that, not only was Calhoun still in town, but he was sitting in the audience.

With a life-size portrait of Kenny and Minnie staring down at her from beside him in the fifth row.

Chapter Seven

Ignore him, Olivia commanded herself. *Don't look at the portrait, either.*

But what mother couldn't look at a portrait of her angels? She'd never had a portrait of her kids before. A few photographs were scattered about the motor home, but still…a portrait.

She sneaked another look.

Calhoun tipped his hat to her.

Minnie and Kenny slid into the seats next to Calhoun, oohing and aahing over their painting. Olivia couldn't hear them, but the joy was clearly expressed in Minnie's round mouth and wide eyes and in Kenny's little shove to get a closer look.

Calhoun grinned at Olivia.

She turned away quickly, focusing on the act. Gypsy shifted underneath her, impatient to begin.

I very nearly missed my cue, Olivia realized. That crazy cowboy was disrupting everything in her life!

And yet, the disruption had felt wonderful—for a moment.

"Nothing lasts, Gypsy," she said. "Let's go!"

They spun around the barrels at top speed, fringe flying and Gypsy's mane bouncing. In and out, they traversed the barrels as the announcer called their names. Briefly, Barley appeared in the arena, bowing to the crowd, then he was gone.

If Olivia didn't know the gag so well, even she wouldn't know where he'd gone. She pulled on her mask with a flourish for the audience, patted Gypsy's blinders and let the horse move forward.

The Star Barrel didn't contain Grandpa, although Gypsy poked her nose in there, then shook her head at the audience, to their delight.

The Flame Barrel didn't contain Grandpa, and Gypsy lifted her head, giving the crowd a big, wide-tooth grin. It was really a lips-pulled-back-from-teeth expression, but she could do it so well, it looked like a cartoon smile.

That left the Sparkly S barrel, and now Gypsy catered to the crowd, prancing up to it and giving it a knock-knock-knock with her hoof.

Grandpa cried, "Ow, ow, ow!"

Gypsy smiled at the crowd again, letting them in on her joke. She stuck her nose down in the barrel, letting out a loud, "Neeeeee!"

Then she cantered over to the other side of the arena, and Olivia took off her mask to pass apples to the kids from baskets that had been placed there as part of the act. Of course, it was Calhoun's side of the audience, so both her children wanted apples, and he reached for one, too, with a whispered, "I was playing, too," while Olivia knew Grandpa was doing the barrel switch.

It was all going to plan except for Calhoun.

Darn his oh-too-sexy smile. It was guaranteed to lure a girl's heart right out of her chest.

Gypsy took an apple in her mouth, walking it over to the Sparkly S barrel. She looked in the barrel, then stared at the crowd. She looked in the barrel again, then back at the crowd.

They called, "He's in the Star Barrel!"

So Gypsy ate his apple, which made everyone laugh. Without missing her cue, she walked over, backed up to it and tipped the Star barrel over. Grandpa crawled out like a spider, running around the ring with great tosses of colored confetti. The children loved it, and Gypsy put one hoof on the Star barrel, posing in a winner's stance.

Gypsy did a side-step routine while stand-in clowns passed apples out to the second side of the arena.

And then everything went eerily quiet. Gypsy stood still. Olivia wanted desperately to lift her mask, which she'd pulled down after the first apple gifting, but she was afraid to spoil the show. Gypsy always knew what to do. It was her act. She would have to rely on the horse to tell her what she needed to do.

Nothing happened for a few moments. The crowd began murmuring, and then gave a loud gasp before applause broke out. Olivia was dying to peek, but she didn't dare. If she did, no one would ever believe that the show was Gypsy's; they would think Gypsy's magic was led by human hands, when, in fact, it was Gypsy's own.

Gypsy moved slightly forward. Olivia tensed, knowing something was wrong. She thought she heard a scuffle on the sawdust-cushioned floor. Maybe a child had thrown something into the audience. Occasionally, someone had a tough time getting all their children settled. But normally nothing rattled Gypsy.

At the final second, when Olivia didn't think she could bear it another moment, Gypsy moved forward.

But she did it more slowly than usual. At the Star barrel, the horse took a longer look than before. She held her pose with pulled-back teeth a second longer at the Flame barrel, for the opposite side of the arena to see. And at the Sparkly S, she knock-knock-knocked with her hoof a bit more gently than normal.

Her explosive neigh was turned down a few decibels as she looked inside the barrel.

"Good horse," she heard a man's voice say. "I like my ladies a little louder, though."

So Gypsy blasted away, before prancing over to the third side of the arena, her gait quite spry, as if she understood that everything was fine.

It was a joke, Olivia realized. Grandpa wasn't in the barrel! "I like my ladies a little louder?" she repeated.

"Pardon?" a man in the audience said to her.

"Nothing," she said hurriedly.

The kids in the audience were laughing. Olivia

didn't dare look behind her, because that would destroy the fooled-you! part of the show. Grandpa should be switching barrels now…except the voice that had spoken to Gypsy had sounded suspiciously like…Calhoun.

Impossible.

"Never saw that other clown do handsprings before," some kid said.

"Must be his replacement," the father said.

His replacement! Olivia's throat dried out.

"Look! Three clowns!" the children cried. "This is the best show ever!"

"Looks like a plain old cowboy to me," the father said. "Maybe the clown had lots of friends to help him out. Nice of them to help him since he's down and out."

Down! Out! It took everything Olivia had not to rip off her mask and go running to her father. *The show,* she reminded herself. *Dad always said the show must go on. Show time is magic time.*

Her hands trembled on the reins. But Gypsy, pro horse that she was, spun into the arena gaily, as if her routine hadn't changed a bit. She went looking for the barrel containing a human, and when the children called out the secret, she backed up to the barrel and ever so carefully rolled it over.

She didn't pose on it this time.

"Good Gypsy," Calhoun said. "That was the part I was worried about. But your horsie-tushie knows how to treat a man right."

Olivia whipped off her mask. "What are you doing?"

"Keep your composure, minx. Your father had a bit of a wayward moment and decided to take a break. He'll be fine in a jiffy. In the meantime, I decided to see if I could save the show. I'm doing pretty good, aren't I?" He gave her a cocky grin. "What a woman you are," he told Gypsy. "Quite the star power in this group. The Mama of Drama, if you will."

Gypsy gave him a grin.

"Your children think I'm pretty cool," he told Olivia. "They're clapping for *moi*."

They were, Olivia saw, the little peddlers for attention. Still, credit had to be given where it was due. "Thank you," she said. "My father wouldn't have ever wanted a show to end on a bad note."

"This one's going to end on a best note," Calhoun told her. "Watch me and this drama queen."

He swung up in the saddle behind Olivia and closed his hands over hers on the reins. "Show time," he murmured in her ear. "Lucky me, I'm in front of the home crowd, too. Gypsy, let's go!"

And go that crazy show pony did, much to Olivia's amazement. Flipping her mane like a tempestuous hoyden, Gypsy went around barrels, winding and dipping, though more slowly because of the extra weight. Giving in to her old training, she danced sideways and then ran another lap.

The audience couldn't stop clapping.

"Stop," Olivia told him.

"No way," Calhoun told her as Gypsy began bowing to the four corners. "This may be the only time I have your fanny between my thighs, and I intend to enjoy every moment of the fantasy. Stop this? I say, let's go, Gypsy!"

The horse began cantering around the ring. Now Olivia was aware of the proximity to Calhoun's... well, his *manhood,* and all her modesty came rushing back.

"I'm getting down," she said.

"You can't leave now. We're just getting started."

"You cannot shanghai me in front of my children," Olivia said stiffly. "Scoot back. You're too close."

"Ah. Only so much room on Gypsy. We'll just have to live for the moment."

Olivia ground her teeth as he squeezed her a little with his thighs. Darn if he wasn't making her think about things she didn't want to! "If I get one hand off these reins, I'm not going to use it to applaud you," she told him.

"Now you're talking my language," Calhoun said, laughter in his voice. "I knew you'd be a foxy lady of pleasure."

Olivia gasped. "I meant I'd slap you!"

"Hmm." Gypsy returned to the center of the arena, posing one last time for the audience, and Calhoun slipped one hand around Olivia's waist now that they'd slowed down. "I've heard slap-and-tickle is fun, but I much prefer to be gentle."

Okay, so she wouldn't slap him, but she was definitely getting away from this lunatic before she completely ruined her reputation, in front of her children, in front of an audience. Sliding down, she curtsied to the crowd.

She pointed to Gypsy, who did her version of a horse curtsy.

And it would be bad manners to ignore the man who'd saved their show. Staring at him rebelliously, she pointed at him in thanks.

The crowd went wild. Calhoun grinned, and in a moment she would never forgive him for, he galloped across the arena, whisked Kenny and Minnie up into the saddle with him and tore around the ring in a victory lap.

He might as well have taken over her whole world, Olivia thought. The crowd *loved* him.

And darn him, she was falling for him fast.

His reward was applause and her children's smiles. Her heart raced in a frightened tattoo. Someone should arrest this man before he lassoed her heart!

The victory lap complete, Calhoun brought Gypsy to stand beside Olivia. He slid down from the horse's back and dipped Olivia backward in a completely showy, unnecessary gesture. When he pulled her back up to him she was spitting mad and bristly like a cat, but Calhoun went ahead and gave Olivia a kiss on the mouth that beat all the other kisses he'd given her so far.

Then he had the nerve to bow to the audience.

She was going to kill him.

"I'M GOING TO KILL HIM," Barley said to Archer and Bandera Jefferson as he lay on his back on a stretcher. "I am going to kill your brother if I have to use the last breath I have on this earth."

"Easy, Daddy-O," Archer told him. "Don't heat your ticker up more than it already is."

"There's nothing wrong with me," Barley snapped. "Except your brother."

Bandera pulled a deck of cards from his pocket. "So, you like cards, Mr. Peppermint?"

"My name's Barley," the clown interrupted. "And you'd best remember it."

"I have a faulty memory. But I do remember Mr. Peppermint," Bandera said fondly. "I loved his little worm friend. What was the name of that worm? You may not have seen Mr. Peppermint since it was a local show." He shuffled the cards on Barley's blanket-covered stomach. "Now, come on, I do believe you're a twenty-one kind of man. When you're feeling better, we'll challenge you at rummy. Not a man alive can beat me at rummy."

"You look like a card player, though not a betting man," Archer said. "Am I right?"

Barley glared at him.

"Well," Archer said, "you've made your feelings about Calhoun plain in the last thirty minutes he's been saving your show."

"Preening popinjay. I know what he's really after. I'd like to snatch him down off my horse and give him a thrashing."

"But you won't," Bandera said, "because you're too grateful to us three Jefferson boys—or did you call us something relating to recently birthed dogs?—for saving your final night in Lonely Hearts Station. And we told the audience afterward that you'd merely had a dizzy moment from some bad huevos rancheros."

"Dizzy moment!" Barley cried with indignation.

"Well, I said you just needed to fart and then you'd feel better," Archer confessed. "That was our father's favorite remedy for everything. And cold water. You remember, Bandera? Dad said cold water was the best medicine on earth for a headache and plenty of other stuff, and if that didn't cure ya, a good f—"

"Now, look here," Barley said, ignoring the fact that he'd been dealt a perfect twenty-one. "I know who y'all are. I know who your family is. I know everything about y'all, because Marvella told me."

"And it's a good thing you've been warned," Archer said with a cocked eyebrow. "Marvella's gossip is as good as those cranky old phones with party lines. Be careful what you overhear."

"I'd trust her more than I'd trust you whelps. Your brother's what gave me heartburn."

"Fart," Archer recommended. "But not until we leave."

"We can't leave yet," Bandera said, reshuffling.

"Not until we tell you how it's gonna be." He put his deck away. "Now see, we're inclined to be reasonable, because we, very strangely, could be looking at having a rodeo clown in the family."

Barley gasped. "Not while I'm alive!"

"Well, but see, you are alive," Archer said. "And you're going to stay that way, because it would matter to Calhoun. Fact is, it's not like Calhoun to hang around a woman. We were so shocked we decided to head over here to check out the scene. Much to our amazement, we find your daughter quite desirable."

"What?" Flame shot from Barley's eyes.

"Settle down, Daddy-O," Archer said, pushing him back down and pulling the sheet tight across him. "Tell the good doctor her patient is ready for his trip to the ward, Bandera. And try not to kiss her. Though she is the hottest doc on the planet," Archer told Barley conversationally. "None of us can even raise her blood pressure, though. We've admired her medical ethics, and we admired her legs. Though Calhoun admires her breasts, as he does every woman's—"

"I'm going to kill you, too, when I get through with this farce of a checkup," Barley said, his jaw tight. "You're all just as insane as Marvella said you were."

Archer winked. Patting Barley's hand, he said, "You want to make friends with Calhoun so you don't lose your daughter, sir. Just in case I don't see you again unless there's a wedding, happy trails."

He left without touching his hat.

"Whew, pity Calhoun for that outlaw being his in-law," Archer told Bandera on their way out. "Hello, gorgeous," he said to the same lady doctor who'd attended all the brothers' various bumps and bruises in Lonely Hearts Station. "Can I have a kiss this time?"

She moved past him without saying a word, going straight to her patient. The ambulance pulled up, the clown was moved to a gurney, and then he was gone.

"It's her hair that kills me," Bandera said. "All that long shiny stuff. I just think a man could—"

"Skip it," Archer said. "Maybe we shouldn't have been so rough on the old man."

"Nah," Bandera said. "A friend of Marvella's is no friend of mine. Plus, it's good to soften 'em up before we let 'em into the family. There is a possibility of that, I suppose. It's not like Calhoun to linger over a woman without a canvas."

Archer nodded. "True. Let's go find Calhoun and his barrel racer. If I hadn't seen her with my own eyes, I would never have understood what had caught his fancy."

"Two more kids," Bandera said with a sniff. "Think I'll get me a vas—"

"Where's my father?" Olivia demanded, nearly knocking them down in her haste. "Where is he?"

"He's fine, and he's gone, traveling by white steel horse to the hospital. My name's Bandera Jefferson—"

But she brushed past him, running back through the breezeway.

The brothers shrugged at each other.

"Welcome to the family," Bandera said to the air. He looked at his brother.

"Hmm," Archer said. "Maybe we should go figure out the lay of the land, for Calhoun's sake."

"I don't like the sound of that."

But they didn't have to go far, because twenty seconds later, Calhoun's truck pulled up in front of them.

"We're headed to the hospital," Calhoun said. "Sorry we couldn't stay."

Archer looked at the barrel racer, her two kids sitting in the middle and his brother at the steering wheel. There was an unwrapped portrait of the kids poking up out of the truck bed.

For what had to be a fast work of art, it was beautiful. Calhoun had caught the kids with a stunning vision of deep understanding. The little girl had on a lovely dress, and she hugged her brother to her, who, Archer would wager, had never been so clean. But their smiles were so real, their faces so completely and truly captured on canvas, that Archer realized nipples were no longer Calhoun's first artistic love.

Bandera pulled the portrait from the back. "Nice. Think I'll take it home so it stays safe. It needs wrapping, but I bet the paint might still be wet. What do I know about acrylics, though? I reckon it's acrylics. Don't know snap about art." He held it carefully.

Archer opened the door. "Come to Uncle Archer, kiddies," he said to Olivia's children. "Uncle, of course, being the friendly term, implying nothing more than I'm the brother of the ambulance chaser," he told Olivia.

Bandera sighed. "About that surgery I was mentioning, the vasec—"

"Uncle Bandera's gonna teach you about roping and I'm gonna teach you how to e-mail Australia," Archer said. "Olivia, your young 'uns will be in the best of hands. We've had twelve in our house to raise and we all raised ourselves just fine."

She hesitated. "I'm not sure—"

"Well, nothing in life is sure. But better with us than being scared and bored in the hospital. We'll take them for some fun."

"Thanks," Calhoun said. "Kenny, Minnie, you're in for a treat. Those brothers of mine, why they're the closest thing to real outlaws—"

"Oh, jeez," Bandera said. "Come on, Mickey and Minnie. Let's go say hi to Delilah and Jerry."

"Minnie and Kenny," Minnie corrected helpfully.

"That's what I said. Penny and Kenny," Bandera stated agreeably. "Let's move on out of Dodge. I feel like some home cooking!"

"I DON'T KNOW if that was such a good idea," Olivia said, watching her kids amble off with the two tall cowboys and the painting. "I don't even know you. I sure don't know your brothers. And what I do know about you isn't completely savory."

"Ah," Calhoun said, a grin on his face. "I suspect your kids, good as they are, will give my brothers new thoughts on avoiding fatherhood and marriage."

"Isn't that what all of you think already?" she asked. "From what I hear, anyway."

"Our reputation precedes us," Calhoun agreed happily. "And it's not always a bad thing to live up to one's reputation."

Olivia could swear he was laughing at her. "That's not particularly amusing to a single mother. Lack of commitment isn't exactly admirable."

"Well, I'm honest. You're honest. We'll get along fine." He patted her knee.

"You're such a bad fibber. I think you want me to chase you. That lack of commitment excuse is a smoke screen. Like playground days of boys-chase-girls and girls-chase-boys. You just want to be chased."

"But not caught," Calhoun said. "Are we having fun yet?"

She rolled her eyes. "Thank you for the banter. It was blasé and fun, but now I want to worry about my dad."

He nodded. "Fair enough. When you're less annoyed and stressed, I'll let you thank me for the portrait. It's not perfect yet, it's not quite what I want it to be, but it is Kenny and Minnie. Did you like it?"

She looked at him guiltily. "I'm sorry. I hardly glanced at it. I know it's beautiful, though. It's just that when I found out the doctor was sending Dad to the hospital as a precaution, I forgot about it."

"Well, Minnie and Kenny loved it," Calhoun said. "I painted Minnie the way she wanted to be painted."

She noticed his satisfied smirk. "Let me ask you something, Calhoun."

"Ask."

Olivia looked at her bare ring finger, then back at the handsome cowboy. "Why do you do so much for my kids?"

"I don't, exactly," he said simply. "I do it for you."

Chapter Eight

The second Calhoun made his reply, he realized he'd erred. Olivia would hightail it if she thought he was trying to get serious on her, and frankly, his ego wasn't looking forward to the rejection. So he went for the too-cool offhand follow-up. "It's our last night around each other. Your kids have been good to me. I like them. What's a little paint between friends?"

Olivia glanced at him. "Paint?"

He nodded. "Paint. It's almost like they gave me a new artistic focus."

"That's all it was?"

"Yes. I really enjoyed trying to bring them to life on canvas, but I'll be sticking to women in the future."

He could almost feel her stiffen. "I see."

"Hmm."

"Naked women?"

He grinned. "Are there any other kind?"

"Apparently not for you."

"Well, threads on a women do distort her better parts. I'm all about bringing beauty to life, you see."

She stared out the window. Silence hung over the truck. Calhoun frowned. Maybe he'd been a bit too free-n-easy on her. Olivia was, after all, a skittish girl.

Then again, it was his experience that the more skittish the mare, the faster they ran if you tried to get near them. Patience was the key.

"So, assuming your dad's fine, where does your act head to tomorrow?"

Olivia sighed. "I'm giving up the act."

"Why?"

"Tonight convinced me. We've been living on borrowed time, although I always thought Dad's knees would be the first to go. This is not a life for a young man, much less an older man." She looked down at her fingers, which she'd clenched in her lap. "I won't say it hasn't been fun. I won't say that this hasn't been a wonderful family experience. We've seen a lot of the country and met a lot of nice folks. Made good friends. But we need to settle down. The kids need to be in school, because I've just about run out of what I can teach them. Maybe not so much educationally as socially. They need to be around kids their own age instead of adults. Maybe once they see how other children act, they'll realize that it's okay not to seek attention all the time. Lots of kids don't have fathers. When they meet other children in the same boat they're in, I'm hoping they'll be reassured." She looked at Calhoun. "I want them to be happy."

"Now wait," Calhoun said, caught by the heavy worries she voiced. "Does your father know?"

"No," she said softly. "But I've known for a while that the show couldn't go on forever. I also know that my father's carried us long enough. A man ought not to have to jump in and out of barrels just because his daughter can't take care of her own family."

Calhoun scratched the back of his neck. "I wasn't sure he was bothered by being the patriarch of your little clan, Olivia."

"Why do you say that?"

"He and I had a little chat last night," Calhoun said, cutting the corners off the real subject matter that had been discussed. "He seemed real happy to be the captain of the ship."

"Told you to stay away from me, didn't he?" Olivia asked.

After a moment, Calhoun nodded. "As a matter of fact, he did."

"Which only made you more determined to hang around." Olivia nodded. "I should have seen that coming."

"What? Seen what coming?"

"I wondered why you painted that portrait. I even wondered what you saw in me, a single mother with two kids. There are plenty of single women hanging around rodeos, hoping to strike up a conversation with a handsome cowboy. And hoping for a little more than that, even. Here you were, painting gorgeous nudes, and I deluded myself for a moment that it was really *us* you wanted."

"I'm doing exactly what I want," Calhoun growled.

"Defying my father. Like your brother is defying his family by running off."

"We have a bit of a defiant streak, I'll admit, but that has nothing to do—"

"I think it does." Olivia got out of the truck as he pulled up in front of the hospital. "A man like you loves a challenge. Loves it long enough to conquer it. And then that's it." She stared sadly into his dark eyes. "It wouldn't matter so much if it was just me. But it matters more because of Minnie and Kenny. You've got to understand. They're not something you can just jump in your truck and drive away from."

He grimaced at the reference to Last. But she shut the truck door before he had a chance to argue.

Actually, there wasn't much arguing to do. What she said was true, in a sense. Barley threatening him had been quite the alluring teaser. In true Jefferson form, he'd wanted to rise to the occasion.

And Olivia was right. Whatever he'd been thinking about her was wrong.

TWO HOURS LATER, Calhoun dozed in his truck in the hospital drop-off zone. One of two things was going to happen, in his estimation: either Barley and Olivia were going to come walking out and they were going to need a ride, or Barley was going to stay for overnight observation, and in that case, Olivia would want to see her kids, and she would need a ride.

He refused to think the old man might have a serious condition. The little family needed Pops.

It was too scary to think Calhoun might have given Barley a stroke or something. He sure did irritate the rodeo clown, and certainly he'd done nothing to alleviate the man's misgivings about him.

Actually, now that he thought about it, a ride was about all he had to offer Olivia and her family—if they would accept his help.

Either way, Calhoun figured a gentleman hung around long enough to offer, though Olivia had made it pretty clear she didn't want him to come inside the hospital with her. Given his conversation with Barley, Calhoun thought he should cool his heels in his truck.

A tapping on his passenger window startled him. He sat up, surprised when Olivia opened up the passenger door and got inside.

"He's going to be fine," she said. "Thank you for waiting on me. I was so worried about Dad, I forgot about transportation issues and getting my kids from your brothers."

"Oh," Calhoun said uneasily. "Uh, you don't need to get the kids tonight. Surely you need some rest."

"I'm fine." Olivia looked at him. "Can you drive me to them?"

"Sure. Would you care to get some clothes? An overnight bag?"

She stared at him. "Why?"

"Well, my brothers weren't certain how long you'd be, and they thought the kids would be more comfortable at the ranch. After they ate a whopping big dinner at Delilah's, complete with cake and ice cream, my brothers took them to get some duds from your trailer, and then they headed out. Archer said the kids were pretty tired, and they fell asleep in the truck on the way to Union Junction."

Her lips stayed parted with surprise. Calhoun mentally sighed, caught by yearning. "You're angry," he said. "I understand, but my brothers meant well. They thought Kenny and Minnie would enjoy the ranch. The dog, the horses, the pond, the swing in the back garden. They're going to fix pancakes in the morning. They didn't want them worrying about their grandpa, and as you said yourself, they're natural worriers."

Olivia didn't know what to say. She was touched, she was concerned and she was annoyed. "They've never been away from me before," she said, voicing her first thought. "They'll be scared."

"They weren't too scared to pass out in the truck. Archer said Miss Delilah fussed over them like mad, and her boyfriend, Jerry, gave them a tour of his eighteen-wheeler. They really liked that. He's got it pretty tricked out. Then my brothers decided, since they hadn't heard from us, maybe they'd better get the kids in bed. Delilah said they could stay there, but we're so shorthanded at the ranch, Archer said they'd best get on."

She decided to shut off her worry valve for tonight. "Thank you," Olivia said simply. "Thank you for caring so much. It's been a very crazy day, and the kids will love being at your ranch. Your brothers are very kind." Leaning her head back, she closed her eyes.

"Are you hungry? Thirsty? Upset?"

"No. No. A little," she murmured. "Dad's going to be fine. A bit more stress than a man his age needs, the doctor said." She sighed, opening her eyes again to look at him. "Calhoun, I'm sorry I said what I said to you earlier. I'm feeling defensive right now. And upset about Dad."

"It's fine. I understand all about family stress. Guess I better pull out of this drop-off zone." He switched on the engine. "I've used up my welcome with the valet." He waved at the man and pulled out of the drive. "So, when are you planning on visiting your dad again?"

"In the morning. Do you mind dropping me off at the trailer?"

"Happy to do it."

Calhoun didn't say another word. He turned on some soft country music. Olivia felt her eyelids drift closed. It had been such an unnerving day! She was so fortunate Calhoun hadn't minded helping out.

If the doctor let her dad out of the hospital tomorrow, she was going to get her kids from Calhoun's ranch, and they were heading home so Barley could rest. Her father would never admit it, but he was tired. Spirit tired. She'd seen it in his eyes as she'd washed the clown makeup from his face.

It was time to bring the curtain down on the act.

OLIVIA WAS SLEEPING so hard by the time he drove the short distance to the trailer that Calhoun couldn't bear to awaken her. She'd wake up soon enough. Leaving the truck windows down, he parked outside the trailer and went to find Gypsy.

The horse whickered when she saw him.

"Oh, I know," he told her. "Everything's fine. Your master's fine. Ornery and still spitting fire. Just not going to get as many opportunities to do it in the future. Your mama's putting him out to pasture. And you, too, I guess." He rubbed her neck. "You deserve the break, you ole show pony. And man, did you ever put on a show tonight. Maybe you knew it was your last one." His hand caressed the length of her nose, making Gypsy toss her head. "I always say it's best to go out with a bang, myself. Now, let me find your hay and fill your water. Tomorrow, you travel to your well-earned retirement."

He filled Gypsy's water, mucked out her stall and tossed in fresh hay. Someone had thoughtfully removed her saddle—probably his brothers. The rule at their ranch was animals first, then humans. They'd probably seen to Gypsy before they went over to Delilah's.

Gypsy pushed at his back with her nose while he picked up one of her hooves to examine it. "What, Gypsy?" he asked, turning to see what she wanted.

Olivia stood there, watching him. "You're up," he said.

"Yes. What are you doing?"

"Chatting with Gypsy." He shrugged. "You were asleep, and I don't like to talk to myself, particularly. I will on occasion, but Gypsy's far more interesting."

Olivia came inside the stall. "I'm too nervous to sleep. My mind won't stop thinking about how I'm going to break the news to Dad."

Calhoun nodded. "News is hard to deliver sometimes. And he's got a ton of pride. Let's presume you don't tell your dad right now. What if you waited awhile? Maybe he could believe he's resting for a few months."

She smiled. "I don't think my dad knows how."

"He'll be learning soon enough one way or the other."

"I suppose so." She glanced over at Calhoun as he picked up another of Gypsy's hooves. "How come you're not married, Calhoun? I know you're running, but it seems like some lady would have set her traps for you by now."

He laughed. "I am an expert at springing traps."

"Grab the bait and go," she said.

"Exactly." Picking up a brush, he began to stroke Gypsy's back. "Your kids ever see their dad?"

She shook her head. "No. It's not something he's interested in, and they accepted that a long time ago."

He glanced at her. "You've got quite a posse of admirers here. They're quite heartbroken that they can't get your attention."

Olivia felt the instinctive twinge of distaste. "I really, really do not want to fall for another cowboy. I can't see trying to fit me and my kids into that lifestyle."

He looked her way as they both digested what she'd said.

"I understand," he said. "Mason tried to keep us off the circuit. It didn't work. Some of us were really good at it, and some of us stunk and one of us never rode a bull or a bronc. It's dangerous, and it's lonely and it's really not conducive to family life unless you're winning a lot. We mainly did it as a crapshoot. We always had the ranch to keep us stable. As stable as we were going to be." He put the brush down, and picked up a hoof pick, gently working Gypsy's back hooves.

"What I like about you is that you homeschool your kids, Olivia. We were homeschooled a bunch. It's good bonding. We went to regular school, too, but what we learned from our folks has lasted longer. Mainly school was a social event for us. Minnie and Kenny know they have a good life."

"I'll send them to school next year, once we're settled," she said softly. "And I'll miss them terribly. But it's time to let go."

She would get a job. It was time for her to become the family caretaker. "Of course, Dad's not going to like me trying to make him slow down."

"You'll have to be very cautious with him. He's got a lot of pride."

Olivia smiled at Calhoun.

"So, where are you from, anyway, Olivia? Where would a man find you if he wanted to, say, drop you a line?"

Her smile dimmed into a regular expression. "The Midwest."

"Now, that was vague." He quirked an eyebrow at her.

"Why would you want to drop me a line?" she asked, her heart feeling that a line would not be near enough from him. She also thought that it was best if he never corresponded with her. "Not that I think you're a letter-writing kind of guy."

"I'm an artist," he protested. "I can express myself."

"But not a writer," she said. "That requires a stamp and a trip to the mailbox."

He put down the hoof pick, took her by the hand and pulled her from the stall. Closing the door carefully behind him, he said, "Say good night, Gypsy."

"Good night, Gypsy," Olivia said obediently, allowing Calhoun to drag her outdoors. He pulled her to his truck and opened the door. She got in, delighted in spite of all her worries that he wanted to spend more time with her.

It would, as she knew only too well, be their last night to see each other.

Still, there had been no "last night" with her marriage; one day it was over. No husband, just a pile of dirty dishes in the sink and an unmade bed. Some old clothes left behind. A note that said, "I gotta go. Tell the kids their dad was good to them. Bryce."

Calhoun started the truck. "First of all, I can afford a stamp, lady," he said. "I even know where it goes on the envelope. And I know where my mailbox is. Even Jeffersons understand the art of correspondence. One of my brothers constantly e-mails a lady in Australia. Other brothers use text messages. One has been known to send up a smoke signal. Or maybe that was an accidental fire. But the message was received," he said with a sideways glance at her. "Your premise is that I won't follow through."

"You are a man," she said unnecessarily, thinking that most men probably didn't write women they'd just met the day before.

"I am all man," he boasted. "And a man knows the secret spots for romance."

Her eyebrows raised. "So, you've mapped out the area?"

He gave her a light tweak on the arm, then captured it to hold in his. "Do not try to ensnare me with slyly couched questions. I promise you I am an efficient trap springer. I have done no mapping around here with females."

"Then how do you know about the romantic spots?" She wasn't sure if she believed his innocent approach.

"My brothers have done their share of mapping."

"And you're merely the cartographer."

He squeezed her hand lightly between his fingers. "It's too bad we don't have longer to get to know each other. I'm certain that a woman who knows a twelve-letter word rarely used in modern-day language is somehow meant to spend more time with me. Slide across this seat next to me so I can rub your legs," he said enticingly. "I have the idea I should be mapping every centimeter of you."

Olivia's eyes widened. "You may be slightly unhinged."

Calhoun laughed. "I may be very unhinged. Come here." He pulled her closer to him on the bench seat. "Now I'm happy. Your father would be mad, but I'm happy."

Olivia caught his hand before it could roam over her knees a second time. "Do you have some issues you need to sort out?"

"Even my issues have issues, Olivia," he said, raising her hand to press her fingers against his lips. "But where you're concerned, I'm very trustworthy and issueless."

She looked at him as they pulled up to a moonlit creek. "This is a nice spot. Very romantic."

He shut off the engine. "Come walk with me."

Opening his truck door, he pulled her out the driver's side with him. "Now, you stand right there and don't move." He closed the door and walked away.

Olivia watched him, a tiny frown on her face. "Where are you going?"

"I'm walking away from you."

"Well, don't. You're worrying me."

Now he was somewhere in the dark and she couldn't see him. "I'd feel better if I had your truck keys!" she called.

"In the ignition," he yelled back. "Feel free to borrow my truck any moment you get the urge!"

Olivia crossed her arms. Okay, the cowboy was playing hide-and-seek. But what was his real game? "Do we know each other well enough to play like this?"

"No," he said, dragging a bench across the grass. "You can get the other side if you want. If not, I can do it myself. I was trying to be the gentleman, though."

"Oh," Olivia said, laughing somewhat nervously. "I thought you wanted me to chase you or something ridiculous like that."

He straightened, and she could see the strong planes of his face in the darkness. "What would be ridiculous about that?"

She stared at him. Shaking her head, she said, "Nice bench."

"Good. Come sit down on it. From this vantage point, we can watch the clouds drift across the moon, just up there. And because it's cold tonight with December's early chill, I get to warm you up." He pulled her into his lap. "Now, you keep your eyes on those soft clouds up there." Moving her hair, he began to kiss along the back of her neck. "I will also keep my eyes up there."

"You're not," she said, laughing. "You sneak."

"They say that fear and sex are a great combination. Is it true? Did I awaken the physical beast in you?"

"No." She turned to look at him. "What are you talking about?"

"You sounded so scared when I went to get this bench. And now I'm kissing your neck. So I wondered if you're having heightened feelings for me.

You know, feelings of gratitude, grateful sex, gratuitous quickies—"

"Stop," she said. "You're crazy." But she laughed at him anyway. "You know what? You're not even trying hard. I finally figured you out. You're all talk, Calhoun."

"Hmm." He shifted his cowboy hat, then hung it on the back of the bench. "You wound me."

"I do not." She giggled and scooted out of his lap to sit at the other end of the bench. "But I do, coincidentally, have feelings of gratitude where you're concerned."

"Yeah?" He seemed to perk up. "Any feelings of sexual—"

"No." She peeped at him with a sly smile. "Well, maybe."

"Really?" He gave a self-satisfied smirk. "I knew you wouldn't be able to withstand my charm."

She shook her head, smiling.

He sighed. "So it's a friendship kind of gratitude?"

"Can you live with that?"

"I think my ego can withstand the pain. So, tell me, and leave out no details, because it sounds like your gratitude's all I'm going to get from you."

"Okay." She took his hand out of his lap, holding it as she turned to face him, one leg crooked onto the bench. "I'm grateful for how you treat my kids. That was an easy one. They wooed you, and you responded in kind. Whether you realize it or not, you were good for them. You could have treated them like kids, or worse, like pests, and they would have been crushed."

"Nah." Calhoun shook his head. "Trust me, those two are wily coyotes. I'm only lucky that they chose me to woo. Because I've sure enjoyed being around them. But don't think I don't understand the game, Olivia. Another town, another man. I'm nothing special."

He said it with such obvious forlorn drama that she rolled her eyes. "No wonder you did so well in our show. You're a master of theater. And that brings me to gratitude number two. Calhoun, thank you so much for saving the show tonight. My kids will remember it always. And so will I."

"So will Barley," Calhoun said. "And that's not an encouraging thought."

"Poor Dad," Olivia murmured.

"Poor me," Calhoun said. "He's going to show me no gratitude at all."

"I'm going to miss you," Olivia said. "Is that weird to say to someone I just met?"

"Not if I made a difference in your life," Calhoun said cheerfully. "And you know, it is said that we Jeffersons do make a difference wherever we go."

He snaked a hand around her waist and pulled her over next to him. "That's better. I was getting cold."

She laid her head on his shoulder. "I'm getting hot."

His posture straightened. "It's about time," he said. "I've been trying to go slow, I swear, but—"

Olivia looked at him.

Calhoun got quiet. "Oh. You really meant hot."

"Yes." Olivia shrugged out of her jacket. "See those clouds up there?"

"Yeah," he said, his tone a little grumpy. "I told you to keep your eyes on them, remember?"

"Not stars, but clouds for us," Olivia said. "I think that's romantic."

"You do?" He watched her, his eyes suddenly intent.

"Yes." She looked up at him. "Calhoun, I'm hot now."

He blinked. She saw his eyes linger on her neckline, and then gaze lower. "My body temperature's moving up, too," he said. "Amazing we both seem to be having the same symptoms."

She smiled. "Synchronicity."

"That's a thirteen-letter word not often used in daily lingo, Ms. Olivia," he said. "And now I'm positive I'm going to have to kiss you."

But she beat him to it, leaning up so that she could get to his lips and wind her arms around his neck to pull him closer to her. Every touch of his lips against hers made her shiver. Olivia felt as if she could drown in the pleasure he made her feel.

I could do this forever.

She pulled away as soon as the thought hit her.

"Oh, no," he said, "no running away. No second thoughts. This time I am going to be the pursuer. You got away from me in the bar, and I let you go then. You want me until I kiss you, but then you start thinking. So babe, I'm going to push all those unworthy thoughts right out of your head."

He kissed her so hard her breath left her, and the worries about forevers that didn't last and fears of not being sexually compatible disappeared like clouds before the moon. Calhoun kissed her so passionately that she moved up into his lap so she could run her hands through his hair and take her time enjoying the heat spreading through her.

"You're hot," he told her. "Sexy hot." His fingers ran under her hair, down her back, and then up the back of her shirt. "Fiery hot mama."

His fingers brushed over her bra under her shirt, and Olivia felt every nerve in her body tense with pleasure.

"Too bold?" he asked her.

She stared down into his eyes. Her nipples were so erect that all she could think about was Calhoun, and making love, which she knew would be different—and crazier—than what she'd known before. She wanted him to make love to her; she wanted him to wash away the bad memories. God, he was so sexy and so manly and everything a woman wanted in a man.

She kissed his mouth, lingering over lips, pressing herself against his hands.

When they broke apart, breathless again, he looked into her eyes. "Am I getting a yes?"

Slowly, she shook her head, her gaze never leaving his. "No."

"Because?" he asked lazily, running his fingers under the back of her bra strap.

"It's been years since I've been with a man," she said simply. "I have no birth control here at Barmaid's Creek." She kissed his mouth again. "And I seem to recall that the Jefferson family is already expecting one unexpected bundle of joy. This is a very bad time of the month to try my luck."

"I—"

She laid a finger over his lips. "Calhoun, before you say something gentlemanly like 'Jefferson men always come prepared' let me just play Pollyanna here and say I'd rather not know that. In spite of how wonderful a man you may claim to be, you do seem to have an amazing knowledge of the female form."

"Purely coincidental," he said, rubbing her back under her shirt. "Those paintings are not women I've known, Olivia."

She felt immeasurably cheered by that. "Still, you can see my hesitation. We don't really know each other, and…while a one-night stand would cure me of a lot of bad memories, it's not really what is best for me. It's not me. The only man I was ever with was my husband." She skipped saying sex wasn't something she'd enjoyed.

He rolled her shirt back into place. "I understand. You're right. Although I want to throw you on your back and take you right here, I do get where you're at. I told myself patience was the key with you, and maybe a little freestyle hard-to-get, but I can also ac-

cept sweet rejection. I think." A sigh escaped him as
his gaze ran across her shirt one final time. "My dad
used to say that the treasure lies within. That's where
yours is, Olivia. I'll miss getting to know you better."

"Thank you," she said, touching his chin lightly.
"If I was going to fall for a cowboy, it might be you."

He held her against his erection, sliding her
against him for just a moment. "If you were going to
fall for a cowboy, Olivia, it *would* be me."

She raised a playful eyebrow. "Maybe."

"It's too bad we don't know each other better," he
said, settling her into his lap so that her head was
against his chest and his arms were tight around her,
"because I would have given you a hell of a memory, babe."

"You did," she said.

And that's the real thing I'm grateful for, she
thought, *but I wouldn't ever want you to know that.*

Chapter Nine

Olivia fell asleep in Calhoun's arms, under the cloud-chased night sky. It was early morning when she awakened to the sun caressing their faces.

Calhoun's arms were still tight around her. Olivia tried to shrug out of his embrace so she could sneak off to relieve herself since there were no accommodations around, but then she realized Calhoun's eyes were open and staring at her.

"Going somewhere?" he asked.

Olivia felt herself blush. They didn't know each other well enough for her to tell him she just needed a quick second behind a bush. "I need to get back," she said, which was true.

"I understand." He sighed, then grabbed her to him for a quick kiss. "Thanks for spending the night with me."

Self-consciously, she tucked her hair behind her ears. She had to look terribly unkempt, nothing like the gorgeous women in his paintings. "You're the only man, besides my husband, that I've slept with, in the nonbiblical sense."

"Well, we are getting somewhere, then."

They started walking toward his truck. "Olivia," Calhoun said, "despite your father's misgivings about me, I do think you should invite me to your home sometime."

She laughed. "You've seen our motor home."

"I mean your real home. I feel awkward letting you walk out of my life like a traveling circus leaving town."

"That's what we are," she said simply. "Traveling, and something of a circus. I could tell you my address, Calhoun, but you'd never visit. We both know that."

He stared at her, and she could tell he wanted to refute her statement. But he didn't.

"You're very busy with the ranch," she said, wanting him to have an excuse, and yet also wanting him to insist that she was not just a traveling attraction that had momentarily caught his fancy.

"Come on," he said gruffly. "Let's get you back to your trailer. I'll call my brothers right now and see what time they're bringing the children back."

She nodded. "Thanks. I need to get over to the hospital and check on Dad. Hopefully, he can go home."

Calhoun made a quick call to his brothers. Olivia sighed, looking out the window while he spoke, then giving in to the urge to watch his lips move while he talked on the cell phone.

He was so handsome.

A second later, he hung up. "They'll be here

shortly to bring Kenny and Minnie right to the motor home. They said the kids have had an absolute blast. Also said they never knew kids could be so much fun." He grinned. "I was a little surprised."

"That's sweet. Thank you."

Calhoun nodded after a moment. "Hey, do you need me to help you pack everything up? Hitch the truck to Gypsy's trailer?"

She shook her head. "We've done this many times. Have it down to an art."

They got into Calhoun's truck. "So, who drives the motor home and who drives the truck pulling Gypsy?"

"I drive the motor home. Dad wouldn't let anyone haul his precious cargo. That horse is practically his best friend."

Calhoun nodded. "One of my brothers has a horse named Curious George that he feels that way about. Curious George is his prize companion. Funny thing, my brother married a woman who was terrified of horses."

"What happened between them?"

He smiled. "Curious George and Navarro went to live in Delaware. They are inseparable, and Nina couldn't bear for Navarro not to have his sidekick. Nina has since learned to love both George and Navarro."

"I like happy endings," Olivia murmured. "Thank you for bringing me back." Her eyes were big as she said, "Thank you for everything you've done for me, and my kids, and even my dad."

"It was my pleasure, Ms. Olivia." He kissed her fingertips to say goodbye.

"I think…I was serious when I said that if I ever fell for another cowboy, it might be you," she said, her heart strangely twisting inside her. This was really goodbye, and it seemed strange that they'd never see each other again.

"Another cowboy?" He shook his head. "It's okay, honey, you can just cross him off your list. You haven't had a real cowboy till you've been a Jefferson's girl. We are the real deal."

She smiled. "Goodbye, Calhoun."

"Bye, my lady."

Hesitantly, her gaze locked with his; she closed the truck door. And then she headed for her motor home to call the hospital.

Although something about Calhoun's turn of phrase—*a Jefferson's girl*—kept tugging at her mind.

Somehow he made it sound so good.

MINNIE AND KENNY sat behind the two cowboys taking them home. They each had a lunch bag to snack from, though the drive was short, only a bit over two hours. Bandera and Archer had given them horse rides, and they'd let them play with the golden retriever, who fetched very well. They'd been allowed to throw rocks into the huge pond out back of the house.

And the Christmas lights strung on the house were amazing. Minnie couldn't stop thinking about all the lights she'd seen. If Santa ever wanted to live at a ranch, she was certain he'd pick Malfunction Junction.

Not to mention the fussy old housekeeper Minnie had barely been able to understand. She'd fussed over Kenny and Minnie, almost like a real grandmother. And they'd eaten something called potato pancakes for breakfast, which Kenny had adored. There was a lady there named Valentine who had baked delicious bread because she worked in a bakery now, she said. Then she'd curled Minnie's hair beautifully and tamed Kenny's bird-perch cowlick, because she said she'd learned how to do those things in a beauty salon a long time ago.

Minnie thought everyone at the ranch was wonderful. "All that ranch needs," she told Kenny softly in the back seat, "is two little kids."

"Huh?" Her brother looked at her funny.

"Did you see all those Christmas lights?" Minnie got a warm glow just thinking about it. "Red and white all over the house. And a stocking for every brother, each one hanging up the staircase. I want a stocking on the staircase with my name on it," Minnie said wistfully.

Kenny looked into his snack bag. "Minnie, a popcorn ball!"

She gasped, looking inside her bag. "I never saw one of those!" Pulling hers out, she stared at it in awe. "I'd rather have this than cotton candy any day," she said, thinking of the spoiled little girl with the pink sugar on her plump cheeks.

"Me, too," Kenny said. "I'm never eatin' it. I'm saving it *forever*."

Minnie thought about that for a minute. "I don't think it would last," she said quietly, "but Kenny, if Momma could just see Malfunction Junction, I bet she'd change her mind about cowboys. I just know she would!"

Kenny's eyes got round. Then he carefully put his popcorn ball back in the paper sack. "You're going to get in big trouble, Minnie," he said. "Momma said no more cowboys."

Minnie looked at the back of Archer's and Bandera's heads. Their hats were big and dusty. But she was used to that. Real cowboy hats looked that way. They were kind. Country music played, louder in the speakers up front. Occasionally Archer sang a little, completely off tune. But Minnie liked to hear him try to sing.

"I bet Calhoun can't sing a lick," she told Kenny.

"But he can paint."

Minnie folded her lips. "I don't think Momma liked that very much."

"Maybe she'd like him better if he sang."

Minnie sighed.

"Hey, Thinker and Stinker," Archer said, turning around, grinning kindly.

Minnie's eyebrows shot up. "Thinker and Stinker?"

"Yeah. You're the Thinker and Kenny's the Stinker, because you two are always up to something. The back seat's too quiet. What are you two hatching back there?"

Kenny giggled. "Minnie wants to live at Malfunction Junction."

Archer looked at her. "You do?"

Minnie nodded solemnly. "I want a stocking with my name on it, just like yours. One for Kenny, too. And one for Momma and one for Grandpa."

"And I want to eat potato pancakes every morning," Kenny said.

"Maybe you should tell Santa Calhoun that," Bandera muttered.

"It won't make any difference," Minnie said. "Momma doesn't like cowboys." She thought about that for a minute. "I don't know why, because Grandpa's a cowboy. He's got lots of horses back home, and a windmill in the backyard. 'Course it doesn't really work."

"Does he?" Archer asked.

"Yeah. But Gypsy's his favorite horse," Kenny said.

"Did Grandpa get well?" Minnie asked, suddenly wondering what Gypsy would do if Grandpa couldn't ride her anymore.

"I think he's much better," Archer said.

"Good." She took a deep breath. "Everyone thinks Grandpa's so mean, but he's not that way at all." Since Archer was still smiling at her, and because she saw such interest in his big eyes, she said, "He reads us bedtime stories every night. And we're the only kids who get to travel in a show. No kid has a rodeo clown for a grandfather, 'cept us." Then she burst into tears.

"Pull over," Archer told Bandera. "Thinker's overheating."

Bandera eased the truck off an exit ramp, parking in a Dairy Queen parking lot.

"Don't cry," Archer told Minnie. "Everything's going to be fine." Under his breath, he said, "Call Calhoun. Tell him to meet us here, because we're stopping for a Blizzard. Tell him not to drag his boots, either." He got out of the truck, opening the kids' door. "All right, Minnie. Come here. You, too, Kenny. We're going to fly in the face of all those parenting magazines Last has been reading, the ones that say comfort food is a bad thing. Let's go get happy the DQ way!"

AN HOUR LATER, Calhoun met his brothers at the Dairy Queen. "Are they all right?" he asked Archer, who came out to meet him in the parking lot.

"They're fine." Archer shrugged. "Worried about their Grandpa."

Calhoun shook his head. "I believe he's going to be fine."

"Believe?"

"Well, without talking to a doctor or getting today's update, I can't say. But last night, Olivia indicated the doctors thought he was suffering from a bit of stress."

"Unexpected stress?"

Calhoun looked at his brother. "Perhaps a little stress brought on by me. We'd had some words."

"And then *we* had words with him," Archer admitted. "Nothing much, just a little 'cool it, dude.' No more, no less than we give anybody else. I'll admit his territorial approach riled us."

"Yeah, he's not the kind of man that would ever change his mind." Calhoun rubbed his chin. "I swear, it seemed like he hated me before he ever met me."

"He did." Archer glanced inside the DQ, where he could see Bandera tossing M&M's into the air and catching them in his mouth, to the delight of the children and a few nearby diners. "Minnie wants to live at Malfunction Junction."

"She does?"

"Yeah." Archer scratched at his neck. "She also says Pops is grossly misunderstood and that his reputation is undeserved. He's a very nice rodeo clown."

"Ah. Under the makeup and attitude is a lamb. I'm not sure I buy it."

"So, is there a thing between you and Olivia or not?"

"Not," Calhoun admitted. "She disliked me before she ever met me, too."

Archer shook his head. "The old man's worried someone's going to take his family away from him, I guess. He's not willing to give anyone a chance. And that's probably been drummed into Olivia's head."

"The thing is, she's crazy about me, I just know it," Calhoun said.

Archer laughed. "Aren't all women?"

"No." Calhoun looked at his brother. "Women get crazy about the ranch, or about what they think a cowboy should be, or our money. But that's what all our other brothers did right—they found women who were crazy about *them*."

"You could always go visit her," Archer said. "Though I think Pops would shoot you on sight."

"Nah," Calhoun said. "I asked her for her address and she cleanly dismissed that. I could tell she didn't believe I'd come her way. That little girl got burned bad when she got burned."

"Yeah, and single moms have different issues. Just like single dads, and brothers who have to become single dads," Archer mused. "No wonder Mason's always been such a pain in the ass."

"Heard from Last?"

"Hell, no. Hey, those two kids in there?" He looked at Calhoun. "Much as I hate to say it, those two have more grit than Last. They're tough little pieces of rawhide, I'll give 'em that."

"Yeah?" Calhoun looked at him.

"They could grow on me," Archer said.

"Funny," Calhoun said. "They could probably grow on me, too." Thing was, he wasn't one hundred percent certain that they hadn't already grown right into his heart.

But with a grandfather who despised him and who might blow a fuse every time he saw him and a mother who didn't want a man in her life, what chance did Calhoun have, except for heartbreak?

"Dude, if you're going to try for it, you're going to have to stiffen up. You're going to have to dig deep and be brave."

Calhoun sighed. "I come from a divided family tree. Half of us winners, half of us wienies when it comes to emotional issues."

"That's right," Archer said. "And those two little kids in there, they need a man who plays on the winners' team."

Calhoun ground his jaw. "I need a Blizzard."

"Comfort the roadside way," Archer said cheerfully. "My advice is you order double M&M's. You're going to need them."

"And you can close your advice column now," Calhoun said testily. "I'm going to call Olivia and invite her and her father to the ranch."

"I admire your game plan," Archer said. "Though I suspect you've lost your mind."

"It wasn't much to lose," Calhoun said, dialing the hospital, "but I feel like being a hero to those kids once again. I sure did like them clapping for me at the show the other night. I got a kick out of their faces when they saw their portrait."

"Good," Archer said, nodding his head. "You just go right ahead and lose your heart. It's the Christmas season. If you fall, the rest of us are safe."

"Who made up that addendum to the rule?" Calhoun said crossly.

Archer grinned. "I did. Because I wouldn't want to be in your boots for nothing!"

"HELLO?" OLIVIA SAID when the nurse handed her the phone. "Calhoun? Is everything all right with Kenny and Minnie?"

"They're fine. Enjoying some R and R with my brothers. How's your dad?"

Olivia looked at the empty bed. "Gone to have an extra test or two run, just to rule out any blockages or other things. It's precautionary."

"So, does he get out today?"

"With any luck." But Olivia wasn't positive. "He's a bit weak, though, which concerns me." Frightened her, actually, but she didn't want to admit it out loud.

"I wonder how good traveling will be if he's not up to snuff."

She'd wondered the same thing herself. "Well, I guess I'll cross that bridge when I come to it. You know Dad. I haven't even suggested he might not be able to drive Gypsy's trailer. And hook everything up." And jump in and out of barrels, and…the list went on and on. Suddenly, Olivia knew her father's world was forever changed. "He can't do it," she said.

"I'd offer, except we're talking about Gypsy," Calhoun said, "the princess of your father's heart. I am the least likely person he'd trust with her."

Calhoun cleared his throat. Olivia sensed his embarrassment.

"I know what you mean, Calhoun," she said. "It's not going to be easy for Dad to realize he has to make some adjustments."

"So, I have an idea," Calhoun said, "which isn't going to go over well with your father, either, but it is something to think about. Perhaps if he came out to the ranch and recuperated, he could give himself a chance to get stronger. Then he would be able to drive the trailer home."

"That's awfully kind of you—"

"Now, I realize I'm the source of your father's anxiety," Calhoun interrupted, "but the ranch is very large, and we might not ever even run into each other—"

"Calhoun, you weren't the cause of anything. It turned out Dad had hypertension he'd never told me about, as well as a few other things he needed to make changes for. He wasn't taking his medication, because he said that damn doctors didn't know anything, and he was just fine. I called our pharmacist back home to see if Dad was allergic to any medication the hospital might give him, and Mr. Finley said Dad had medications he never picked up that the doctor called in for him."

"Whoa," Calhoun said. "That's not good."

"No, it's not. Now, Mr. Finley couldn't tell me what the prescriptions were for, of course, but he gave the cardiac doc here the name of Dad's doctor so they can discuss Dad's case. It's going to be fine. But you'd think he'd at least take the medicine he's prescribed."

She'd been startled, actually, by the chain of events. They were all lucky he hadn't had a heart attack. Or worse. "You know, Dad's too stubborn for his own good."

"I can't comment on that, exactly, because I'm from a long line of stubborn men. It's really to our disadvantage to be as ornery as we are, but it seems to be a gene thing."

"Well." Olivia felt as if her chest was heavy with worry. "I hope Minnie and Kenny have been good."

Calhoun glanced through the DQ window. Archer had gone back inside, and now both of Calhoun's brothers were teaching the kids sign language—with a few Gig'ems and Hook'em Horns thrown in for their greater education. "I say come on out to the ranch for a bit," Calhoun said. "Give your dad a chance to get his strength back. You'd like it, I think," he said. "Minnie does."

Olivia laughed. "It must be good then."

"It's a no-strings-attached offer," Calhoun said. "No fair, no foul, nothing but a house to yourself and a place for Gypsy to hang with some horse friends."

"You make it sound so easy," Olivia murmured. "We can't just pull up with a motor home, a trailer, a truck, two kids and a sick man."

"Think about it," Calhoun said, "but from the sound of things, you'd fit right in to Malfunction Junction."

"I have to go," Olivia said suddenly. "They're bringing Dad back in, and Marvella's here with a bouquet of flowers."

"Ah. Beware the dragon bearing gifts," Calhoun said.

"That's not how the expression goes," Olivia told him.

"Close enough," he said. "Call me after you talk to the doctor. There's no point in bringing the kids back to Lonely Hearts Station when they're perfectly happy at the ranch. You can't watch the kids while you're at the hospital, anyway, and they'd be bored stiff. And worried. Jeez, Olivia, these kids are always nervous."

"I know." She was a bit stung by that. "Calhoun, thanks. I'll call you as soon as I know something."

She hung up, staring at Marvella. "Thank you for coming to visit Dad."

"Actually, I came to talk to you, though I also brought these for the ole coot."

Olivia narrowed her eyes. "Ole coot?"

Marvella took off her wide-brimmed, Sunday-special hat, carefully dusting the bright flowers off as she set it on the bed. "He is. He's old, and he's a real sonofa—" She stopped herself and looked at the empty bed. "So, he's not dead, is he?"

"No." Olivia glared at Marvella. "He's gone for some tests."

"Good." Marvella appeared relieved. "I hated to think he might be turning up the daisies when we hadn't had a chance to really talk."

"What do you need to talk to Dad about?"

Marvella shrugged elegantly, perching on the bed,

looking every inch the royal madam. "Old times. Good times. And proper goodbyes."

Olivia blinked. "What's the point?"

"What's the point to you letting a Jefferson hang around?"

Olivia raised an eyebrow and crossed her arms. "That's none of your business. Calhoun has been very good to me and my kids."

Marvella laughed. "That's the game," she said, "and they play it so well."

"Look. Why have you really come here?"

"To chat with the old man before he leaves town. I thought he'd visit me, but he didn't, and so, as they say, the mountain must—"

"Maybe he doesn't want to see you."

"He does. He's just busy with his family, and he's not certain how he'd be received. We had words a long time ago. I'd like to put the past to bed."

Olivia stared at her. "I'll tell Dad you stopped by."

"Good." Marvella rose from the bed. "Here's a free piece of knowledge from me to you. Jefferson cowboys are the sexiest men on the planet. Their dad must have been a real piece of work, because there's not a woman who can keep her panties on around them. I can't catch them doing it, but I know my girls even slip them into my salon from time to time. They're fun, they're loose and they're wild, and no woman can resist that. Don't try to catch a stallion that can't be broken." She put her hat back on, setting it carefully on her curls.

"Why the free advice?" Olivia asked.

"Because you're Barley's daughter." Marvella turned to look at her. "I never wanted to tell you this, because I thought one day he would tell you himself." She took a deep breath. "You're also *my* daughter."

Chapter Ten

Olivia felt as if her world had fallen apart. Yet the expression on Marvella's face told her she was telling the truth. "I don't understand," Olivia murmured.

"We were married. We had you. My sister, Delilah, stole my husband, and I've never forgiven her for that," Marvella said bitterly.

Olivia frowned. "Dad's never mentioned a woman named Delilah. I knew you and he had once been sweethearts, but he never mentioned another woman."

Marvella frowned. "Delilah wanted to steal you away from me. She never had any children of her own. In the end, we both lost you and Barley."

Olivia realized she was trembling and sat down on a chair. "I am telling you, Dad never mentioned he was married. I never knew who my mother was. Dad was all I ever had, so I never asked many questions. That's why Minnie's constant questions about everything always surprise me. She's so different from me."

"Well," Marvella said. "I don't know what else to say, except that I hope the ole man is fine. Of course, I never got over him," she confessed, her voice sad. "I'd like to kill him for dumping me that way. I should also say that you've turned out quite well."

"How did I end up with Dad?" Olivia could hear her voice shaking.

"He took you back home to his ranch. He had the money, so he had the rights. Maybe deep inside myself I knew you'd be better off with him."

Olivia couldn't understand why her heart wasn't glad or relieved to discover this missing piece about herself. "I think you should go now."

"I will." Marvella moved to the door. "You asked about the free advice. Let me just point out the obvious. If you got tight enough with Calhoun to get married, he'd be related to me, after a fashion. And I think you should know one thing—the Jeffersons may ride for me in the rodeo occasionally, for charity reasons or for the challenge, but there is no love lost between us. Honestly? The number one reason you'll never win Calhoun…is me."

With that, Marvella swept from the room. Olivia gasped with pain, her mind racing. Why hadn't her father ever told her?

It all fell into place. They'd never performed the act in Lonely Hearts Station. This was a one-shot, never-look-back, going-out-on-top goodbye. Dad wanted Marvella to see him in all his glory before the curtain came down for the final time. Maybe he even wanted her to see how good he'd done raising their daughter alone.

Her father was wheeled in and transferred to his bed.

"Howdy," he said. "Thanks for the flowers."

She looked at the blooms Marvella had left behind. "Enjoy," she said.

"Damn doctors. I want out of here."

"Soon, Dad, soon." She couldn't say anything more.

He looked old and somehow fragile. Tired. She wanted to scream, wanted to force him to answer her questions, but he needed as little stress as possible.

"Ms. Spinlove?" the doctor said.

"Yes?"

"A word, please."

She followed the doctor into the hall. "How is he?"

"We won't know the test results for a couple of days, but my preliminary diagnosis is that your father has a heart condition, brought on by wear and tear, and taking too little care for himself."

Tears brimmed around Olivia's eyes.

"He needs to be very careful," the doctor continued. "Aggravating this is not a good thing. He needs to change his life significantly."

Olivia shook her head. "Did you tell him?"

"I did. He cussed me and told me to butt out of his business. Said he had a daughter and two young grandkids to care for."

Olivia drew herself up straight. "No, he doesn't," she said sternly. "From now on, we'll be taking care of ourselves."

FIVE MINUTES LATER, Olivia kissed her father good-bye, tucked him in and hurried outside. She dialed Calhoun on his cell phone. When he answered, she said, "I've just finished talking to the doctor. Where are you?"

"We're still at the DQ. Somebody's kid here tried to imitate Bandera by catching M&M's in his mouth, and somehow got one stuck up his nose. Now, I'm not sure how that can happen, but kids can do anything, I guess, and Archer's about to perform the Jefferson on him."

"The Jefferson?"

"Oh, yeah. We used to get things stuck up our noses all the time," Calhoun said. "Well, it never happened to me, but pea gravel seemed to be the biggest culprit for my brothers."

"Eww."

"Yeah. Anyway, after a couple trips to the emergency room, we had the procedure down pat. He's just gonna blow in the child's other nostril—"

"Calhoun. That's good, thanks. No more info, please." Olivia grabbed a taxi at the curb to take her back to the motor home. "I'll meet you there to get the kids."

"Going home? Dad getting out of the hospital?"

"Too soon to tell. But I'm coming to get Kenny and Minnie, so don't move."

"But—"

Olivia hung up. Her intuition—that she and Calhoun didn't belong together—had been right from the beginning. He could be habit-forming. The last thing she wanted was for him to know her secret. Even after such a short time in his company, she knew how much the brothers despised Marvella.

Beware the dragon bearing gifts, he'd said.

This time she'd been bearing a doozy.

"OLIVIA," CALHOUN SAID when she pulled up at the Dairy Queen, "slow down and talk to me. I want to know about your father."

"No," she said definitively. "I've leaned on your kindness long enough."

He frowned. Her hair was wild, her eyes were wilder. "What's wrong?"

"Nothing." Olivia gave him a blank look. "Kids, say goodbye to the Jeffersons and get in the truck."

He watched her closely as the kids said goodbye to all three of them, then got inside the truck as she asked.

"Was it the M&M story?" he asked. "I swear, it came out just fine. The mother was entirely grateful. And your kids never dreamed of shoving any color-ful round chocolates up their noses."

"No," Olivia said. "Everything is fine. Thank you so much for all your help."

"Here's the portrait," Bandera said, carefully plac-ing it in the truck bed. "Bro says it's not finished, but he'd need more time to work on it. I think it's pretty good, though."

Olivia allowed a small smile to cross her face. "It's more than you should have done, Calhoun. Thank you."

And she got in the truck and left, the kids waving out the window to him.

"Damn," Archer said, "did a tornado just tear through here?"

"That was weird," Bandera agreed. "Even for a worried woman, she was knotted up good and tight."

"Yeah," Calhoun said. "More skittish than ever."

"Don't know if those flighty ones work out too well," Archer opined. "I like 'em calm myself. 'Course, I like 'em best when there's no kids involved, even though those were pretty sweet kids."

Bandera sighed. "You're not the subject matter here. Olivia and Calhoun are."

"There is no Olivia and Calhoun," Calhoun said. "Because unless I'm wrong, she just told me to buzz off."

"Did seem so," Archer agreed. "Felt like the ole heave-ho to me. Don't think you own a lasso long enough to rope that running filly."

"Maybe you should go after her," Bandera suggested. "Ask her what her problem is."

Calhoun shook his head. "When a woman has her foot down on the gas pedal that hard, she doesn't want to be asked any questions. C'mon, boys, I'll follow you home."

Still, he stared into the distance after Olivia's truck.

Archer sighed. "Wienies never win."

Bandera put his boot up on the truck bumper. "Something blew her skirt up. Don't think you quite had her locked down, bro."

Calhoun rubbed his chin. "Maybe the news was worse on her dad than she thought. He despises me, so maybe she figured not being friendly with me would help her dad get better."

"Yeah…" Archer crossed his arms and leaned against the truck. "Had you kissed her properly?"

"And then some," Calhoun said.

"She seem happy about it?" Bandera asked.

She always seemed happy when she was in his arms, Calhoun mused. "We got along fine that way."

"Then it's something else." Archer put on his wise face. "When you talked to her, before she called and said she was coming here, what did she say?"

"She said she had to go, that Marvella had just come in with a bunch of flowers—"

"There's your answer," Bandera said. "Anybody care to argue with me?"

The three brothers looked at each other.

"No," Calhoun said slowly, "don't think I would." It all made sense.

"Marvella told Olivia what a womanizer you are. She told her that Valentine was pregnant and Last wouldn't marry her, that we're irresponsible oafs with little-boy mentalities—" Archer began.

"She knew all that," Calhoun said, "and still she slept in my arms the other night at Barmaid's Creek."

"I do love our reputation," Bandera said cheerfully. "We're like every father's worst nightmare."

Calhoun shook his head. "It wasn't the rep."

"Well, we won't figure it out standing here," Archer said. "I say we follow that speeding truck."

"Spying's my favorite thing to do," Bandera said. "Actually, my favorite thing to do is thwart Marvella, and I sense that's going to play in here at some point. I can be patient and wait."

"I suspect Marvella did throw down the gauntlet," Archer said. "Please do say you're not having a wienie attack, Calhoun. We haven't picked up any gauntlets lately, and besides, it's just plain fun to torture Marvella."

"Nope, no wienie here," Calhoun said, settling his hat on his head. "For the sake of those kids, I'm feeling like a winner."

Of course, it was more than that. What he wasn't about to tell his brothers was the essence of what no man ever wanted to admit: he was falling in love.

Despite all the reasons not to fall for Olivia Spinlove, he was pretty certain he needed her in his life.

"That barrel-racing mama needs me," he told his brothers.

"Like a hemorrhoid," Bandera said with a grin. "Let's pony up."

AN HOUR LATER, from the comfort of the pavilion, they watched Olivia pack things in the motor home. Minnie and Kenny carried boxes and bags, and Olivia secured them wherever they belonged.

"She's leaving," Calhoun said, his heart heavy. "Soon."

"Like ASAP," Bandera agreed. "You're gonna have to work fast if you want to catch her."

"But what would he do if he caught her?" Archer asked. "There's so much baggage. Are you ready for that much baggage, Calhoun? Most of us travel pretty light. Sometimes we don't even carry a suitcase. Did Last have a suitcase on his motorcycle? I doubt he did," Archer said, answering his own question. "You will note that the greater our desire to leave emotional baggage behind, the lighter we pack. There is a direct correlation."

"So what does that say about all that stuff 'n gear the little lady's got?" Bandera mused. "Motor home, trailer, truck, bags, boxes…I never saw so many belongings."

"Lot o' problemos," Archer said.

"Both of you shut up," Calhoun said. "There is no correlation between the size of your bag and your emotional receptivity or availability."

"Go talk to her," Bandera said. "If you feel like you can handle her gear. More power to you. If not, leave her alone." They watched Olivia run her hands through her hair tiredly, then sit on the trailer stoop with her kids. "Don't mess with her unless you're willing to go the distance, bro. That one's traveling heavy."

Calhoun shook his head slowly, his eyes feasting hungrily on Olivia and her children. "I can paint myself into that picture just fine, thank you," he said. "Watercolor, acrylics, oil—it doesn't matter. I see us in any medium."

Archer squinted at the small family. "From nipples to 'us.' It's almost too much to contemplate, and yet, so…so…Calhoun," Archer said. "Not to get too personal here, but if you had to do a painting of Olivia, and you were going to do her nude—"

"Watch out," Calhoun growled.

Archer cleared his throat. "Well, could you paint her breasts? Her…you know. Nipples? Your favorite body part?"

"Is a nipple a body part?" Bandera asked. "Isn't it a part of the whole?"

"Calhoun considers it in its own most special category," Archer said. "There is an existential side to my questioning."

"Really?" Calhoun briefly took his eyes off Olivia. "Which is what?"

"Have you seen them?" Archer asked defiantly.

"I have not," Calhoun said sternly. "She's a lady."

"Well," Archer said, folding his arms, "that tells the whole story. You've gone over the edge for a woman without caring what she looks like under her shirt." Archer shook his head. "There's only two ways this can end—either you marry her, or you say goodbye and remember the one woman you fell for with her shirt on."

Calhoun turned back to watch Olivia. "Everything about her is fine. She's brave, and she's fun. She's cheerful, and she's a good mother. She's sexy. My pants stay on fire when I'm around her."

"And all that without ever seeing her naked. Boy,

you're going up in flames if you ever get with her," Bandera said. "I'm convinced she's the woman for you. Cover me, Archer, I'm going in."

"Wait!" Calhoun exclaimed, striding after his brothers as they approached the trailer.

The kids saw the men first, running for them as fast as they could with delighted yells. Olivia didn't get up from the stoop. She watched Calhoun approach without smiling.

"What are you doing here?" she asked.

"We were worried about you," Calhoun said. "We didn't know how you were going to pack up the motor home by yourself, or Gypsy, the kids and your dad. We wanted to make you an offer," he said, with only a half-apologetic glance at his brothers. "Once your dad can travel, we think you should let us drive you home."

Chapter Eleven

Olivia stared at Calhoun, only mildly aware that Archer and Bandera were leading her kids toward town. "Drive us home?"

"Sure. Your dad can rest in the motor home. Archer's the king of horses. He and Gypsy would get along fine. I'll drive the motor home, and you can hang with your kids and take care of your dad."

His offer surprised her. "I don't think I can do that," she murmured. "Though you're sweet to suggest it."

He sat beside her on the stoop and tucked her hair behind one ear. "Olivia, did I do something wrong? Have I upset you?"

"No," she said, hating to see the disappointment in his eyes. She couldn't tell him the truth. And yet, the hurt was clear in his eyes. He didn't understand why she wasn't treating him as she had before.

She could tell him, or not tell him, the choice was hers—but not telling him meant he would never think less of her. By the shine in his eyes, she knew he admired her.

It felt so good to be admired by a man as wonderful as Calhoun. "I like you, cowboy," she whispered. "I really do. I can't say yes to your offer, and I can't see you anymore, but I really, really do think you're the best man I've ever known, besides my father."

"Hmm," Calhoun said. "I'm not sure that's a ringing endorsement."

She squeezed his arm. "Don't take it wrong. You're both wonderful. You make me dream dreams, Calhoun."

"What kind of dreams?" he asked, staring hungrily at her lips.

"Those kind of dreams," she whispered. "The kind you're thinking of right now."

"Olivia," he said. "Why did you leave like that?"

"Reasons I can't tell you," she said. "Things that happened long before you and I met. Calhoun," she said, putting her hand out for him to take, "come with me."

He slowly rose, never taking his eyes from hers. She drew him into the motor home and locked the door. "I don't want to leave you without saying goodbye. I don't care what my father thinks, or anyone else. For some reason, when it comes to you, I don't even care about my promise to myself."

"Oh," he said, pulling her up against his chest, "never break a promise to yourself."

"I had promised," she said, rubbing her hands lightly over his chest as he held her, "never to fall for a cowboy."

"Well," he said, picking her up and settling her legs around his waist, "that one you can break."

He kissed her, and she went breathless. She could feel him hard underneath her, and Olivia welcomed the knowledge that she'd be a lot happier woman if she let Calhoun into her life. Even if it was just for this night, she deserved this man.

"You make me whole," she whispered against his mouth as he carried her back to her bed.

"You make me want the entire thing," he said, tearing off his shirt and then hers. She tugged off her jeans, and she did the same for his. When she was down to matching blue underwear, he took a deep breath. "Come here, Olivia," he said. "Don't keep me waiting a second longer."

Her eyes huge, she went into his arms, staring up at him. "I'm…not scared," she told him.

Silently, he laid her on the bed, covering her with his body as he found her mouth. He kissed her— long, hard, deep, and for five minutes—before he spoke. "How's the fear factor now?"

"I'm not scared," she said.

"We're not ready until you say you are. I never want you to say that word again." He ran a hand down her hip, tugging her up against him. He kissed her slowly, passionately, patiently for at least another five minutes. Then he looked into her eyes. "How are you, Olivia?" he asked, his voice deep as he caressed her bare thigh.

"I want you," she said. "I want you so much, Calhoun."

He pulled down her panties, moving them over her feet and tossing them to the floor. Very slowly, he removed her pretty blue bra and cupped a breast. "Tell me again," he said, squeezing a nipple lightly. Then he kissed her nipples, one then the other, sweeping a hand up the inside of her thigh.

Olivia arched, her fingers tugging him anxiously to her. "I do. I want you."

He raised his head to nibble at her lower lip. "You're sexy," he told her. "You're hotter than the firecrackers we set off in Shoeshine's barn when we were kids."

"What?" She could hardly think. Calhoun's hands and mouth were driving her mad.

"Hot," he said huskily. "I've wanted to get inside your heat since the first second I laid eyes on you. But you're going to have to want me, Olivia, because when you remember me, you're going to remember me with a smile on your face."

"Calhoun," she said, nervously realizing she might not be able to convince him that she wanted to make love with him. "I want you. I want you to make love to me. I want you to hold me, and kiss me, and…I want to hold you inside me," she finished, not knowing how else to convince him that she would never be afraid of him, that she truly hungered for him.

He slipped a finger inside her, finding her wetness, and Olivia gasped. But he was over the edge now, and determined to take her with him. He kissed every inch of her body, before licking up inside her. Olivia held back a scream as her body was taken over by sensations she didn't understand, like strings pulling her toward heaven, and just as she thought she was going to come apart from the pleasure of the magic he was bringing her, he entered her. Then she did scream, clutching him to her as he covered her mouth with his, taking her cries of joy inside him.

And then Olivia realized she had never experienced true marriage before. "Oh, my gosh," she said, when they lay in each other's arms ten minutes later. "Calhoun…I—"

He rolled his head to look down into her eyes, and she went silent. He was so handsome, so manly. Everything about him was strong, and kind, and gentle. He was the Elusive Sexy Cowboy she'd run from, and yet he was the man of her dreams.

Dreams Marvella had crushed. Her eyes dimmed with the memory of that conversation. There was so much she couldn't say to Calhoun.

"Tell me," he said. "I want to know your every thought."

She smiled shyly at him. "I think you're handsome. And I think you're good at *that*." Then she blushed.

"Hmm." He rolled over to bite at her neck lightly. "You're keeping secrets, and that's a number one no-no."

"Okay. Um, I'm hoping I compare favorably in your eyes to the women you paint."

He drew back to stare at her face, her nipples, her

navel and her most private area. She could hardly bear his scrutiny, and she tried to pull the sheet up over her, which he caught in one hand as he lightly moved a hand over her hip. "I will paint you one day," he said. "But you won't be nude, because no one is ever going to know what's under your jeans but me. In fact, I'm giving up painting nudes for life. I have my favorite nude right here."

Her blood chilled. He sounded so serious. As if they were going to be together forever.

"So tell me," he said huskily, "before I have to give you the old-fashioned lie detector test."

She smiled. "What?"

"I can tell if you're fibbing," Calhoun said. "A man has a very precise and delicate instrument to gauge his lady's honesty."

"He does not," she said, laughing, until he slid inside her, just an inch. "Oh!"

"Now," Calhoun said, kissing her lips, "this is the most reliable way for two people to get to know each other. It's very accurate in testing honesty, as well."

She stared at him, wanting badly to wriggle so he'd move farther up inside her. She tried to, but he shook his head. "Uh-uh," he said. "You can't be so forward. You tell the truth and I reward you."

"No," she said. "You're driving me insane, Calhoun."

He nibbled her ear. "Olivia, do you like me?"

"Yes," she answered immediately.

He moved an inch farther inside her. Olivia

groaned and tried to pull his hips but he grabbed her wrists and held them over her head. Then he kissed her nipples, taking a long turn with each.

"Olivia," he said, after licking his way up to her lips, "you ran off on me today. You *ran*. And it wasn't a good thing, because I felt like I'd hurt you in some way."

"No, you didn't, I promise," Olivia said, and he rewarded her by sliding inside her another inch. Olivia arched, her breath coming faster. "Calhoun, please."

"Is it your father? Because I think given time, I can work out a better relationship with him. I'm willing to try," he said.

"No…Calhoun, there was nothing wrong. I think I just felt like I'd imposed on you and your brothers," Olivia began, but he pulled back an inch, and she looked up at him, startled and feeling empty.

His gaze was determined.

"I can't tell you," she finally whispered. "It's my personal business. But it had nothing to do with you."

He began filling her up again, and Olivia squirmed, wanting him so bad.

"The truth?" he said.

"The truth," she replied. "Nothing to do with you at all. I got a little spooked."

It wasn't the complete truth, but she couldn't tell him that. He seemed satisfied after he studied her eyes for a moment, then he stroked her with determination, possessing her as his alone, and Olivia felt the difference in his movements and his passion.

He'd been gentle before, working through her fear, but now he was her lover, believing he could keep her safe from anything.

Olivia cried out with pleasure, and Calhoun followed her into her bliss, and as he whispered her name over and over in the dark, Olivia knew she was going to lose the best man, the only man, she would ever love.

Chapter Twelve

Calhoun left the trailer an hour later, with Olivia sleeping like a contented cat. What he loved best about her, he decided, was how innocent her face looked when she slept. She was sweet, Calhoun decided, and his former shadowy misgiving must have been his wild side giving one last call to him before he pushed it away for good.

Olivia was his woman, real and in the flesh, not a painted lady.

"Foxy and fine and all mine," he said happily, heading over to the Lonely Hearts Salon. Whistling, Calhoun found his brothers and the children over at Delilah's, eating pancakes.

"These kids are spoiled," Bandera said. "They talked Delilah into making them their favorite food."

Delilah laughed. "It was no trouble. How are you, Calhoun?"

"Never been better," he said, which made his brothers laugh. He glared at them as Delilah handed him a heaping plate of pancakes. "Where's Jerry?"

"On the road. Left yesterday." Delilah sat down with a cup of blackberry tea. "I have never understood how that man can drive such a big rig, stay gone a week and only take a couple changes of underwear and an extra set of clothes. He packs so light."

Bandera and Archer looked at Calhoun.

"And that just shot your emotional baggage-size of suitcase scenario," Calhoun said cheerfully. "No correlation at all."

"Where's Momma?" Minnie asked, her lips wet with syrup.

"She went to the hospital to check on your Grandpa. Gypsy says to tell you hello," Calhoun said.

The kids giggled.

"When Gypsy says hello, she usually does it by tapping a barrel with her hoof," Kenny said.

"Or giving you a nudge with her nose," Minnie added.

"Well," Calhoun said, "this time, she said hello by sneezing all over my shirt."

The kids thought that was funny. Delilah smiled at him. "You planning on making something of this?" she asked.

"I don't know." Calhoun shrugged. "Not sure the lady in question is appropriately eager."

"Really?" Bandera asked. "We figured for sure you'd lock her down this time. What are you waiting on?"

"I don't know," Calhoun said, his good mood

evaporating. "Just a moment ago, I felt great. But now that you've put a fine point on it, I'm not sure. Guess I don't want to talk about it."

"No one's talking," Archer said.

"It's just that she's a secretive little thing," Calhoun said, thinking out loud. "She says she's telling the truth, but I can tell something's still bothering her."

"Women are delicate creatures," Delilah said. "We like to be able to figure things out ahead of time. We don't like things out of order."

"Calhoun's definitely out of order," Archer said. "He fell before he looked at what lay below."

Calhoun sighed and drank his milk. "This is delicious, Delilah."

"Thank you. I'm always glad when the Jefferson men stop by." She smiled at them. "You know, speaking of things that are out of order, my sister, ever-peculiar Marvella, has been even more peculiar lately."

The three brothers looked at her, pausing in their eating.

"Well, it might be nothing," Delilah said. "But she stopped me on the street the other day, and she asked me if I'd ever regretted not having children. Of course, I said I'd been lucky to have all these girls come to my salon who needed a job and a new start. Truly, they are my sisterhood and maybe my parenthood. But then she said the biggest regret she'd ever had was not knowing her child." Delilah shook her head, sipping her blackberry tea. "She's gone off her rocker, you know. Marvella never had a child." She sighed and sat back in her chair.

"Then she said she was enjoying the charity work I'd gotten her into. Remember when she needed a bull at the last rodeo, and I lent her Bloodthirsty, but made her promise in exchange that she'd do charity work?"

The brothers nodded.

"Turns out she likes it." Delilah smiled. "Maybe it will make a difference in her life. It's good to care about the people around you, instead of just caring about how to make a fast buck."

The brothers hastily dug back into their pancakes.

"It was quite strange, though," Delilah said. "Marvella and I quit speaking after her husband left her. She thought I'd stolen him. But nothing could have been further from the truth, which she has managed to twist over the years. Oh, he did come to see me once or twice, but it was on matters of business, and nothing more than that. Let's see, what was his name?" She looked around the table, then at the pancakes. "Barley," she said. "His name was Barley."

Calhoun quit eating to stare at her, as did Archer and Bandera.

"My grandpa's name is Barley," Minnie said.

"It is?" Delilah said. "Goodness, not many people have that name, would you think?"

"No," Calhoun said, thinking rapidly. "No. Oh, no."

"Oh," Archer said, with a glance at the children, "that would be too bad."

"Ye gods," Bandera said, his napkin dropping

from around his neck as he looked at Minnie and Kenny. "You don't suppose?"

Calhoun's throat dried out. The children looked up at him, smiling, their eyes innocent.

"Oh, no," he said. "Life wouldn't be so cruel."

TWENTY MINUTES LATER, Calhoun had Kenny and Minnie at the hospital to meet their mother. His brothers had returned to Union Junction, somewhat glum for his sake.

But he wasn't worried. There was no way that Marvella, the woman who had tried to sue Malfunction Junction through Valentine and her coming baby, the woman who was capable of more twists than a pretzel, could possibly be related to the Spinlove family.

It was out of the question that Marvella would ever be related to the Jeffersons.

"That would make her my mother-in-law," Calhoun muttered. "Which is too scary to contemplate."

"What?" Minnie asked.

He looked at her. "Thinker, do you have any family besides your grandpa?"

She shook her head. "Momma always said we just had each other." Her smile was big. "It was enough, though, Grandpa always said."

Calhoun's heart beat uncomfortably. "Hey," he said, squatting so that he was resting on his haunches and looking up into Minnie's and Kenny's little faces. "You're good kids," he said. "Real good kids." He stared into their eyes, trying to articulate his feelings.

"Listen, when my brothers and I were growing up, we were hell on wheels. We got into all kinds of trouble. Shoot, we thought we invented new twists on trouble. That's why they call our ranch Malfunction Junction. But if we'd been half like you kids, we would have turned out better people." He reached up and touched each of their cheeks. "You're good kids, and don't you ever forget it."

Minnie's little mouth turned down a bit. "You ain't keepin' us, are you, Calhoun?"

He watched a bit of brightness flood her eyes. His heart ached.

"Calhoun?" she said. "I was kinda hopin' you wanted to be part of our act."

His chest felt tight. "Minnie, honey, you've taught me a lot about loving the whole more than the part. Being around you and Kenny and your mom made me realize I wasn't painting the whole picture. But..."

"But you can't be our father," Minnie said simply.

He closed his eyes for a moment. How could he explain that her mother didn't want to settle down, and there were reasons for that? Most particularly, she didn't want to settle with him. And if it were true that Marvella was their grandmother, there was no way in hell he was going to be the Jefferson who brought her into the family tree.

They'd have to put a lock on the henhouse if Marvella was around.

"I can't, Minnie," he said slowly. "Not that you wouldn't be wonderful children to be a father to, and

I want you to know that." He shook his head, his heart breaking. "In my family, we have an old superstition. Do you know what a superstition is?"

"Something you think will make something happen to you. Like, Grandpa never eats before a show cuz he says it'll make him sleepy." Minnie smiled. "Grandpa's never sleepy during a show."

Calhoun nodded. "It's something like that. Well, in my family, we believe in a silly thing called The Curse of the Broken Body Parts."

Minnie and Kenny smiled.

"I told you it was silly," Calhoun said. "Only this time, it doesn't seem so silly. You only get cursed by the broken body parts when you've fallen in love, and each one of my brothers has hurt something when they met their future wife and family."

"Didn't you break anything when you met us?" Minnie asked.

Slowly, he took their hands in his. "Turns out I did," he said softly. "My heart got broken. Which is why I know there'll never be a little boy or a little girl I love as much as I do you two."

They put their arms around his neck and squeezed.

"It's okay, Mr. Calhoun," Minnie said. "We'll be all right. As Momma always says, the show must go on."

OLIVIA GLANCED UP when Calhoun walked her two children into her father's hospital room. "Thank you for bringing them," she said, hugging both her children.

"Mr. Spinlove," Calhoun said, politely tipping his hat.

"Hmm," Barley said.

"I hope you're feeling better." He turned and met Olivia's eyes. "Olivia, can I have a word with you?"

She got up and followed him into the hallway.

"How's your dad?"

"Going home today. The doctor says he's well enough to travel, but he needs to avoid strain and difficult conditions."

"Olivia," he said heavily. "How are you going to get all of you back home? To…where is it, anyway?"

"Kansas," she said. "Not so far. We'll be fine. We've managed before."

"Your father can't drive Gypsy's trailer. He needs to rest. Does the doctor know what you're planning? I'm pretty certain he'd advise against it."

"We'll be fine," she said, but even inside herself she wasn't certain.

"Where do the kids ride when you're driving?"

"Usually in the truck with Dad."

"Well, not this time," Calhoun said. "At least promise me that. What if he has a heart attack, Olivia? Are you thinking this through?"

Anger flared inside her. "I would never endanger my children."

He held up his hands. "I know you wouldn't. But I don't think any of this is a good idea."

"My life is my own," she said. "Just because something happened between us, doesn't mean—"

Before she knew what had happened, he'd grabbed her hand and dragged her down the hall into a small break room. Closing the door, he pulled her close to him. Olivia's heart pounded.

"What exactly happened between us, Olivia?" he asked. "Yesterday you went cool on me. You took off like a cat out of a cannon. I made love to you, and I gave you time to tell me what was wrong. But you didn't. And now you're off again, without so much as a goodbye. I spent more time saying goodbye to your kids than you'd give me."

"I don't know what to say," she said. "Honestly, Calhoun, I don't. I didn't mean to fall for you, I didn't mean to sleep with you and I didn't mean to hurt you."

"But?"

"But we're just not right for each other. And we both knew that in the beginning. I live in Kansas, you live here. My family travels, yours stays in one place, for the most part."

"When they're not avoiding something? Like their responsibilities? Is that what you were going to say?"

"No," she said, stung. "Why would I? If anybody is avoiding their responsibilities, it's me."

He let go of her. "What do you mean?"

"I spent time with you instead of here with my father. I spent time with you instead of with my children. My horse, my packing—I haven't done anything except be with you."

"Do you regret that?" His face was hard.

"No." She shook her head. "But I know it's time for me to quit spinning daydreams and get back to reality."

"Reality doesn't include me."

She shook her head in the negative.

"You're a tough cookie, Olivia Spinlove. I see now where you don't fall far from the tree."

She felt her face flush. "What does that mean?"

"I don't know," he said softly. "Maybe you should tell me what it means."

"If you're saying my father—"

"I'm saying your mother," he said pointedly.

He knew. She wasn't going to tell him, but he knew. What was worse, he also knew she had planned on leaving him without telling him the truth.

"How did you find out?" she asked.

"So it's true?"

"Apparently so. I haven't asked Dad yet, and I'm not going to because he's not supposed to get upset. It's a talk that can wait." She looked at him defiantly. "It's bad luck for me, maybe, but it doesn't change anything. Not really."

His jaw tightened.

"I am sorry," she said more gently, "but Calhoun, you said yourself you weren't much interested in more than the surface of a woman."

"I never said that."

"Sure you did. You love to paint women, but you don't paint women you love."

He stared at her.

"I was never going to fit into your heart," she said sadly. "Let's not pretend. If I had fallen for your cowboy shtick, you would have hit the gas as fast as Last did."

"That's it," Calhoun said. "I'm taking you home."

She pulled away from him. "What are you talking about?"

"No woman," he said, "and I mean no woman, accuses me of not having a heart. You're going to bring the traveling circus to the ranch."

"I cannot. We planned on being home by Christmas."

He smiled at her, but it didn't seem his eyes were happy. "Guess what? Christmas comes to Malfunction Junction just the same as it comes to Kansas."

"What's the point of this?" She glared at him.

"Because," Calhoun said, "you're the original runaway gypsy. I should have known that a lady with a horse named Gypsy, who lives in a motor home that stays on the road, would be all about roaming free. But Ms. Spinlove, you just ran out of run. Your kids need me, and they need stability, and they're coming home with me for Christmas."

Chapter Thirteen

Calhoun's cell phone rang. He pulled it out of his pocket, clicking it on. "Calhoun," he said.

"Best come on home, Calhoun," Crockett said. "We have a baby on the way."

Calhoun blinked. "A baby?"

"Valentine's having her baby. Any idea where Last is?"

"No, the son of a gun." He looked at Olivia, thinking hard. "How long do I have?"

"Could be several hours. The doctor says first births usually take the longest."

"I'll be there. I have a matter to settle."

"Spinlove matter?"

"Yeah." Calhoun opened the break room door into the hallway so Olivia could leave, but she stood watching him.

"Hey," Crockett said, "not that it's any of my business, but I'm about to have a Christmas stocking made for Valentine's baby, because it will be a Jefferson." He coughed. "Seemed like those Spinlove kids mentioned something about liking stockings with their names on them."

Calhoun watched Olivia watching him. What was he going to do with Marvella's daughter? "I imagine they would."

"Could send them up to their house for Christmas," Crockett suggested.

"Excellent idea. Thanks for thinking of it. I'll be home soon." He hung up. "We're having a baby, so I'm going to have to get. Make up your mind, Olivia. Pack Pops up and bring him to our ranch for the first leg of the journey, or let me drive you home to Kansas."

"Calhoun, there's no reason—"

"There's every reason. Listen, Olivia, you remember how you warned me about your kids and how they always wanted attention?"

She nodded.

"Well, now they're getting it. Real attention. I'm him. Mr. Attention."

"You don't have to be," she said.

"Yeah, I actually do," he told her. "I'm not sending you, a sick old man and two little children off on the road. It's a dumb idea, but I understand where you're coming from, because we have dumb ideas all the time at Malfunction Junction. Only difference is we always have somebody around to dig us out. We have each other. On the road, you won't have anyone."

"All right," she said slowly. "I see your point. Thank you for offering your hospitality."

"So which is it? You come to me or I come to you?"

"We'll come to Malfunction Junction. Just until Dad rests a bit."

"Good." Calhoun looked at her. "But don't worry. It's a no-strings-attached offer."

"So…"

"So I'm doing this for your kids, Olivia."

OLIVIA WATCHED Calhoun walk out of the break room, his big strides carrying him away from her. His words rang in her ears, leaving her breathless. Once before, he'd told her that he helped her kids because he was really doing it for her.

Now he was saying it was all about her kids.

It was the first time she'd seen him with any sort of anger in him, but now it was there, and she couldn't blame him. She'd hurt him. Dishonesty was never a way to touch someone's heart. And he didn't appreciate her not needing him.

He had tried very hard to be patient and kind to her. She shivered, thinking about how sweetly he'd made love with her.

Even before Marvella's disastrous confession, she had been planning to leave Calhoun behind without even a forwarding note—and he knew it. He might not have known it before, but he did now. He called her a gypsy, and she had to think he knew her better than she knew herself.

Now he had a reason not to want her, and it hurt. Maybe she'd meant to leave with him still wanting her, so that she would always feel desirable when remembering her onetime fling. Maybe it was true that what someone once did to you, you eventually did to someone else, as a way to heal yourself.

Only she didn't feel healed. She felt broken.

The only way to make up to everyone for her actions was to start over. It was too late for them now. Even she knew that this race could not be rerun.

It was too late, because he no longer wanted her. Her relation to Marvella, as Marvella had predicted, was the final tearing between them. But more than that, she'd always had one foot propping open the door so she could shove him out at any moment.

She had, he'd gone, and now they were finished.

But he loved her kids, and he intended to do good things for them, even if it meant putting up with her and Dad and Gypsy and a motor home and everything else that came along with their act.

Everything about her was an act, she realized.

She'd been acting all along as if she didn't care, when she cared more deeply than she could ever admit.

She went down the hall, realizing that she needed to have a long talk with her father. Minnie and Kenny came running out the door, meeting her in the hallway.

"Where are you going?" she asked them.

"Mr. Calhoun says we need to scram for a minute," Minnie said. "And he gave us money for ice cream in the cafeteria."

"Hang on a sec, and I'll walk you down," she said. "Sit right on that bench over there until I check out…everything," she said, meaning Calhoun.

To her surprise, Calhoun was in Barley's room, shaking her father's hand.

"Now, I know you don't like me, sir," Calhoun said, "and I certainly don't like you. Man to man, I think that's a fair-and-square starting point. Personally, I'd rather someone tell me to my face that they hate me than act like they like me right before they bury an axe in my back. So, zero is fine with me."

"What else?" Barley said, as Olivia hovered in the doorway, listening shamelessly.

"As a representative of the Jefferson family, I'm inviting you to our ranch to stay awhile, maybe a week, till you get your feet under you. It's for the sake of Minnie and Kenny that I offer, because it's Christmastime, and they deserve better than being broke down somewhere on a cold highway with a sick old man and a woman and a horse."

"You know, son, I don't like you," Barley said. "Don't like you a bit."

But he said it without depth, Olivia realized, and that meant he was listening.

"That's fine," Calhoun said. "As I said, all I'm interested in is sharing the Christmas season with your grandkids. Can you do better right now, old man?"

There was silence for a moment. Barley said, "Well, I could, but the doc says I can't. Of course, he doesn't know his ass from a goat, but I've got to go with his orders or he says I'm gonna end up on the wrong side of a grave."

"Well," Calhoun said, "you seem fit enough to

me. But doctor's orders are just one more thing to live through. You'll be fine in a week, I imagine, and able to cart your family home."

"So, what about my daughter?" Barley said gruffly.

"She says she thinks she can get you home herself."

Barley humphed. "Stubborn."

"Well, I know. So it's up to you to convince her that while you're obeying orders, you might as well sit and see a working ranch while you have the chance."

"Working ranch?"

"Yes, sir," Calhoun said proudly. "That's what we are."

"I thought y'all were just a bunch of leftover candy-ass dime-store cowboys living off your daddy's money."

"That, sir, would be a rumor."

"Marvella told me that. She runs the—"

"We have acquaintance with Marvella. We have a love-hate relationship. We love to hate each other. It's a good relationship and benefits us all when we need it to. Something similar to what I'm proposing to you."

"Hmmph," Barley said. "I don't like you."

"I'm not worried about it, Barley. Let's get this thing agreed to, because I've got a baby on the way, due to make a delivery any moment now."

"What?" Barley exclaimed.

"Well, not my baby, precisely. It's my brother's,

Last's. But he's not around, and that means we all step up to the plate. Actually, it doesn't matter whose baby it is, because Jefferson men don't forget what's right."

Barley sighed. "I may have misjudged you."

Calhoun glanced over his shoulder, catching Olivia eavesdropping. "I'm going to go hitch your trailer," he told her. "Why don't you see about dismissal papers for your dad. I'll pull around front. You have two options. You can drive your motor home and stay in that as you do now, and I'll drive Gypsy's trailer, or you can drive Gypsy, and I'll cart your crew home in my truck. You can stay in one of our smaller houses on the property. Your choice. Either way, we're only a couple hours away if you've forgotten something."

Olivia blinked. "Dad? What would you like best?"

Barley's eyes grew big. "To be honest, and as much as I hate to admit it to this contrary individual, I am tired of living on the road. I am fairly sick of our motor home, and it does seem to me that, if it's not putting you out, a real house would be a wonderful place to stay for the Christmas season. But only for a couple of days," he warned.

"Only until you're feeling stronger," Calhoun agreed. "We'll get you gone as quick as we can. I promise."

He glanced at Olivia, his words for her, then left the room after she handed him their keys.

"Whoa," her dad said. "Did you two have a row?"

"No," Olivia said carefully. "We're just not interested in each other."

Barley wrinkled his nose. "Then why is he doing all this if he isn't an egg-sucking weasel trying to get into my good graces so he can be my son-in-law?"

"I don't know," Olivia said softly, picking up the flowers Marvella had brought her father and placing them in the trash. "I forgot to tell you that those flowers were from Marvella."

"Oh." He looked surprised momentarily. "Why would she bring me flowers?"

"I guess because you took sick at the rodeo," Olivia said carefully. "Maybe that's how they do things here."

He scratched his stubbly beard. "I guess. So, where's that crazy cowboy? And what did you decide about all our vehicles?"

Olivia blinked. Her father didn't seem either concerned or impressed that Marvella had been by to see him. Then again, her father was a wonderful actor who had been working audiences for years. "I'll drive Gypsy, because we can unhitch the trailer and still have a vehicle for us to use."

"Mom?" Minnie said, poking her head around the door. "You promised us ice cream, and we've been waiting patiently—"

"Oh, my gosh. Dad, I'll be right back." She went out the door, catching up to the kids. "Now, listen, you two can't take money from Calhoun in the future, okay? He was just being nice this time, but—"

"Mom," Minnie said, stopping in the hallway. "Please don't worry so much. We're not asking him for money. We're not asking him for anything. We remember the rule."

"No cowboys," Kenny said. "We're being good."

Olivia hesitated, staring down at her two beautiful children. Children she loved more than anything in the world. They did try so hard to be good.

"We were hoping for a father, but now we understand Calhoun is not the one," Minnie said. "He only broke his heart when he met us. To be our father, he has to break something more important."

"Like an arm," Kenny said. "I think."

"What?" Olivia looked at her children in their mismatched clothes, with their messy hair that hadn't been combed, and their eager-to-please expressions.

"It's okay, Momma," Minnie said. "We understand it all."

Olivia followed her children down the hall. Had anything in her life ever hurt this much?

She had thrown away the one person who loved her children the way she'd always dreamed a man would.

And he'd tried to love her, too.

AN HOUR LATER, Calhoun pulled up at the hospital, driving his truck, with Gypsy's trailer hitched to it. He'd forgotten Olivia would need clothes for the whole clan. This way they could leave their truck behind, and Olivia could drive the motor home.

When they were ready to leave, they could just get

in their motor home and drive away intact, with Gypsy hitched to the back. Complete, like a turtle carrying its house on its back, they could take everything with them.

Not that he'd be happy about it, but he knew it was best to plan for that eventuality.

He went inside. Barley was sitting in a wheelchair waiting by the front desk. "Ready?"

"Am I ever," Barley said. "Let's hit the road."

"Okay. Where's the rest of the crew?"

Olivia came around the corner with her children, chocolate-ice-cream smears around each child's lips.

"Good," Calhoun said, "you've had dinner."

Minnie and Kenny giggled.

"We're ready," Calhoun said. "Are you?"

"As ready as I'll ever be," Olivia said. "Thank you, Calhoun."

He waved her thanks away. "All right, Barley, let's spring you." Wheeling him to the curb, he said, "For the short ride to the motor home, you can ride up front with me. Olivia, you can sit in back with your kids."

Everyone moved to where he suggested, and he helped Barley into the truck, without seeming to really help him.

"I'm good," Barley said gruffly.

Olivia and the kids looked at Calhoun from the back seat. "Ready?" he asked.

They nodded, and he closed the door.

He got inside the truck, and they headed away silently.

When he reached the motor home, Olivia said, "Since you have Gypsy hitched to your truck, are you thinking I should drive my truck?"

He met her gaze in the rearview mirror. "If you take the motor home, you'll have all your stuff with you."

"True," she said.

"And you can leave whenever you all decide you're ready."

Her eyes widened. But he kept his gaze firm.

"Okay," she said softly. "Kids, let's get into the motor home. Luckily, it's all packed and ready to go."

Calhoun helped Barley inside.

"Ah," the rodeo clown said, "it feels good to be out of that hospital. Though they were nice people. Except for the doctor, who was opinionated."

Calhoun laughed. "Follow me. We'll be home in no time."

The kids got into the motor home, digging around for their crayons and coloring books to take on the road. They stretched out in their bed so they could see out the window as they drove.

"Good to go," he told Olivia, who seemed to hesitate before she got in the driver's seat.

"Are you sure you want to do this?" she asked.

"It's the best thing, until your father feels better."

Olivia looked up at him. "I don't want to be a favor to you. A responsibility."

"You fall somewhere above that, Olivia."

"I see." Turning away, she got behind the wheel.

"Follow me," he told her. "Be sure you buckle up."

"I will."

He closed her door, drawing a deep breath. Okay, now he had the whole family under his wing.

He wondered why that made him feel so good.

Yet somehow apprehensive, too. The same way he felt when he was rodeoing, right before his bull crashed out of the gate.

Chapter Fourteen

Olivia's breath caught as they pulled up to Malfunction Junction. The ranch looked like a fairyland with beautiful, twinkling lights and decorations. No wonder her children had been so entranced. "It looks like a Christmas card," Olivia murmured.

Calhoun's home looked like the house every cowgirl imagined in her dreams.

"Nice," Barley grunted as he leaned on her arm. "Quite the spread."

"Mmm." Olivia wasn't worried about that. She was more concerned about the details she had to clear up with her father at some point. When he was feeling stronger, she intended to ask him to tell her the truth.

It was killing her. She couldn't stop thinking about it.

"Doncha like him, gal?" Barley asked as they went inside the door of what Calhoun called the "second house."

"Dad, there are reasons people aren't meant for each other. Calhoun and I have plenty of those."

"If it's because of me," Barley said, groaning a bit as he eased into a lounger below some impressive buck antlers and a large fish on the wall, "me and Calhoun have come to terms."

"It's not because of you, Dad," Olivia said, not wanting to talk about Calhoun right now. Talking about Calhoun was not going to improve the situation. Sometimes, people couldn't go back in time. Maybe if her dad had been more welcoming up front, maybe if she hadn't been so afraid of relationships, maybe if Marvella wasn't her mother— "The world is full of maybes," Olivia said. "Maybe I should go unhitch Gypsy and put her in her new pasture."

"You do that," Barley said. "I'm going to get forty winks."

"Good idea." Minnie and Kenny had run up to the main house because Calhoun said gingerbread men were out on the table, freshly baked by Helga, the housekeeper.

To her surprise, Calhoun had already unhitched the trailer from the motor home and was now leading Gypsy out.

"Thanks," Olivia said. "You didn't have to do that."

"Yes, I did. Gypsy said she was ready to go make friends." He walked her toward a paddock and let her through the gate. The horse turned to look at him once, before ambling off to find a good yellow grassy patch.

"Thank you," Olivia said, "for everything."

"No problem." Calhoun handed her the lead. "I've got a baby being born. I'll see you tomorrow. Call the main house if you need something—Helga can help you."

Olivia's gaze followed him as he walked away from her.

Her heart pleaded to go with him, to be included in his world, but she knew the time for that had passed.

CALHOUN FELT BAD leaving Olivia that way, but he'd promised her that this would be a no-strings situation. He'd said he hadn't brought her here to seduce her. His word on that was ironclad.

"Mason called," Bandera hollered down from the second-story window. "We've got a baby!"

"What is it?"

"A little girl. Valentine's naming her Annette, because she liked Mimi's name for Nanette so much."

Made sense. Women thought that way. He liked the name Minnie, though.

She came peeling down the hall when she saw him.

"Calhoun! There's a baby born on the ranch!"

He laughed and tugged her hair. "Not on the ranch, honey. Annette was born in a hospital. But she's part of our ranch now."

"I want to be part of your ranch," she said. "And so does Kenny."

Calhoun smiled. "You two run on down to your Mom now. I think she's looking for you now that she's settled your Grandpa. Take her a gingerbread man. Or woman. Gingerbread person."

"Okay." They ran into the kitchen, then went whooping out the back door.

"What are they so excited about?" Archer asked as he came down the stairs.

"The baby. The cookies. Christmas. What aren't they excited about?" He went to get a celebratory beer out of the fridge before he went to see Valentine's addition to the ranch.

"Dude, they're making me excited, and I wasn't." Archer grabbed a beer, too.

"They're easy kids."

"And the mom?"

"Not so easy," Calhoun said. "We sort of split our feelings down the middle and called it quits."

"Too much too soon?"

"Too little too soon. I can't bring Marvella into the family, and that's the thing that weighs on my mind."

Archer shook his head. "It's a crying shame."

"Everything's a crying shame. Like Last not being here for his baby being born. We do the best we can."

"Yeah."

They sat in silence for a few minutes.

"She watched you, you know, walk all the way over here."

"Who?" Calhoun looked at his brother.

"The little barrel racer. From the window, I could see she never moved from her spot."

Calhoun shook his head. "It means nothing. We both know where we stand."

"Do you?"

Calhoun nodded and then put down the beer he'd barely sipped. "Let's go see the newest member of the family."

Archer got up to follow him. Calhoun shook his head in silence, thinking of all the things the brothers had gotten wrong lately.

Suddenly, he frowned. "How did Mason take the fact that Mimi's selling her ranch?"

"We haven't told him yet. We were waiting for you to come home so we could have a family conference."

"Thanks."

"The family that shares each other's pain, shares each other's gain."

Calhoun grunted. "Let me know when there's been gain where Mason's concerned. Personally, I think he's slid back into his old ways."

"Yes," Archer said, "but sometimes shocking news about the woman you love brings your slide skidding to a halt."

"Tell me about it," Calhoun said dryly.

OLIVIA SETTLED THE KIDS into their new bedroom, which they loved. "Gypsy likes her pasture," she told them as she stroked their hair away from their faces. "She told me to tell you that she wants you to come see her tomorrow."

"We will, Momma," Minnie said.

"Momma," Kenny said.

"Yes, dear?"

"Do you wish we could stay here forever?"

The smile slipped from her face. "Well, no, honey. We have our home in Kansas."

"Yeah." Kenny closed his eyes, relaxed under Olivia's fingertips.

"But we have no cowboys at our place," Minnie said. Her eyes flew open. "Sorry. I know I wasn't supposed to say that."

Olivia smiled. "It's all right."

"I meant, I'll miss Calhoun. And everybody here. They're awful nice to us," Minnie said earnestly.

Still worried, even about upsetting her mother. "Go to sleep, honey," Olivia said. "It's fine. You relax and have sweet dreams. Everything is fine now. Grandpa's fine, and Gypsy's fine, and I'm fine, and you're fine."

Minnie closed her eyes, then opened them briefly as if checking to make certain her mother's gaze still reassured her. Then she sighed and shut her eyes again.

Olivia shook her head. She had told her children that it would be all right, but her definition of all right and theirs were different. She knew exactly what they wanted—and she knew they would never have it. It wasn't something Santa Claus could bring them—love only came maybe once in a lifetime.

Quietly, she turned off the lamp, leaving the night-light on, and went downstairs. Her father was reading a fishing magazine.

"Howdy," he said. "I swear I think I'm feeling better already."

"Really?" She sat down across from him. "Maybe you just needed a vacation."

"Yeah. Maybe that's it." He squinted at her. "It's nice to have someone else taking care of us for a change. No wonder old geezers move in with their kids when they get old. I feel like I'm living at a palace!"

Olivia shook her head. "Palace pass runs out in a week."

"Not if you get married to that young fellow," Barley said slyly.

"Dad!" She was so surprised, she started laughing. "Dad, I can't get married just so you can live like a retired king. I'm surprised at you."

"Nah, I was just teasing. It's not my style anyway." Barley flipped a page.

"Dad," Olivia said, not feeling like laughing anymore. "Calhoun isn't the marrying kind. At least not for me."

"You told me. I heard ya. I still say if that's the case, why's my fanny sitting in his rocker?"

"Well, he's being nice, for one thing." Olivia sat up straight. "Dad, why didn't you tell me Marvella was my mother?"

Slowly, he closed the magazine. "Because I didn't think it was wise. She didn't want to be a mother. And I thought that was a bad tail to chase. A woman who doesn't want to be a mother isn't likely to change, honey."

Olivia's eyes filled with tears. "It's not that, exactly. I never thought much about not having a mother. I was fine with our life like it was. But...the second Calhoun figured out Marvella was my mother, he completely lost interest in me. I mean, I didn't exactly help matters myself, but that was the point of no return."

"How does Calhoun know?" Barley demanded, frowning.

"He figured it out himself somehow."

"And how did you figure it out?"

"Marvella told me when she came to your room."

He looked stony. "Busybody."

"Yeah." Olivia looked down at her interlaced fingers.

"So you think your cowboy backed up a few paces on you because he doesn't want Marvella in his family tree? Not that I can blame him, but—"

"There was some lawsuit she brought against them, or helped bring against them, and it had something to do with the baby that is being born tonight. It's one of the brothers, only he left, and...I don't know," Olivia said. "Apparently, Marvella causes lots of problems for the Jefferson brothers."

"Well, Marvella could cause a rhinoceros problems, but I don't see why it should affect you. It's not like either you or Marvella are going to take a shine to the other and start writing each other letters. Or calling to discuss recipes over the phone. What does it have to do with Calhoun?"

"The lawsuit. They wouldn't want her to think of

another way to get her fingers in the Jefferson pie. If she's my mother—"

"Ah. And quite a pie it is. I see their situation. Still, you shouldn't be blamed for your parents, either her or me."

"I don't think Calhoun's worried about you. But financial matters are another issue. No one's going to threaten their ranch."

Barley's eyebrows beetled. "Well, there's not much we can do to change who you are. I'm real sorry about it, but a fact's a fact. All you can do is understand how he feels about it and move on, I suppose." He sighed heavily.

"Yes." Olivia rose. "I love you, Daddy," she said. "I'm going to get you some tea. I saw they had some wonderful choices in the kitchen."

"Thank you," Barley said simply. But as his daughter left the room, he watched her, a worried pucker between his eyebrows.

Chapter Fifteen

"Hey," Calhoun said the next morning around 5:00 a.m., when he realized Olivia was sitting on the stoop of her motor home. "What are you doing up?"

"I always wake early," Olivia replied. "Country habit, I suppose. What are you doing up?"

"Ranch habit. Have to take care of the beasts. And I wanted to check on Miss Gypsy. But I can see she's content."

"How's the baby?"

Calhoun grinned. "A Jefferson beauty."

Olivia nodded. "I would never have thought otherwise."

"Nice jacket." He looked at the large plaid wool coat she was bundled into, a coffee cup beside her.

"Thanks. I think it's yours."

He smiled. "Looks better on you."

She looked off into the distance. "It's quieter here than I thought it would be. So restful."

He leaned up against the motor home. "Only because just about everybody except Helga is still in bed."

"No, I mean, it's quiet. Peaceful."

"Christmastime silence. The waiting period," he said. "It's sure not this way in the spring. The grackles and mockingbirds will get you up before the sun does."

"Poetic," she said. "The waiting business, not the grackles."

"This is my favorite time of year. Sometimes I just sit and look at the house."

"I couldn't have guessed from all the lights you have strung. What's your electric bill like during this most wonderful holiday?"

Calhoun laughed. "Plenty. But worth it. This is the only time of the year where all the family comes back home. Unless there's a wedding, and everyone definitely comes home for that."

Olivia looked away. "So," she said, "my dad's taken a shine to your fishing magazines. He says he's totally relaxed."

"Fishing magazines will do that to a man." He patted her knee, then got up. "Well, chores are calling. See you later. Let the main house know if you need anything. Breakfast is on at six but if you can't make it, there's always something on the sideboard. And the kids are welcome to whatever they want in the fridge. Or cereal. We don't eat it, usually, except on weekends, when we give Helga a break. Try to, anyway."

"Thank you."

He nodded. "Are you all right?"

"I'm fine."

"You seem quiet."

She shook her head with a smile. "Just enjoying the solitude."

He'd be willing to bet she hadn't had many times of peace and quiet. He wondered if she knew how cute she looked in his jacket, with her fingers around his coffee mug for warmth. "Enjoy," he said, heading away.

"Calhoun," she called.

He turned. "Yeah?"

"I asked Dad. Marvella is my mother."

Too bad, he wanted to say. But he just looked at her. "Are you okay with that?"

She shrugged. "It doesn't really matter. She didn't want to know me then, she doesn't want to know me or my kids now. It's not like my life has changed significantly."

Yeah, but he'd bet she was still absorbing the shock of meeting her mother face-to-face. He wondered how soon he'd recover if he ever saw his father again. When Mason had finally returned earlier this month, Calhoun had felt as if someone kicked him in the stomach. He was glad Mason was home—but he wanted to beat him on the noggin for leaving. So many feelings had hit him—and probably all the brothers—that they all just ignored the situation, instead of hammering Mason as they should.

He wondered if Olivia had sorted through her feelings yet. "Don't reckon you'll ever tell Minnie and Kenny?"

She shook her head. "It wouldn't be a good thing. They've had enough worries. It would hurt them to know she wasn't interested in them."

Whew. So many betrayals for such short lives. "Tell them I'll be back later to get them," Calhoun said. "We're going to run out for some fun. With your permission."

"It's fine. They'd love that."

"About twelve."

"I'll have them dressed."

He looked at Olivia one more time, noticing her hair lay softly over the jacket collar and seeing that her lips were a little chapped. He was struck by an urge to do something about that, but a promise was a promise, and one should always keep his promises, especially ones made to himself.

He loped off, still not believing that he could have the incredibly bad luck to fall for a woman who was related to Marvella.

Especially since he couldn't stop thinking about how wonderful she felt, how sweet she tasted and how beautiful she was naked.

Nudes. Always his favorite thing. But now he only had room in his heart for one nude. His brushes had gone dry; his paint hadn't been touched. He'd quietly nabbed the portrait he'd started of Minnie and Kenny and planned to finish that in his spare time over the next week.

But what he really, really wanted to do was make love to Olivia again.

That was something that would never happen. It would be like saying that her runaway heart and her family ties didn't matter. It would be like following his heart over Niagara Falls in a barrel. Caution to the winds.

It would be unfair to her.

But he wanted her, as he'd never wanted anything before in his life.

And maybe that was part of his attraction to her. She was the one thing he couldn't—shouldn't—have.

"NOW THIS," CALHOUN SAID that afternoon when he had the kids with him. "*This* is a birdhouse."

Minnie frowned at the gourd. "It looks like a squash."

"Yes, but certain birds love to make their homes in them. It doesn't matter the shape or size of a home—it just matters that the birds find it just right for them."

"Like our motor home," Kenny said.

"Exactly." Calhoun went up the ladder. "Now the important thing to remember is that certain birds feel this is the farthest south they can fly for the winter. So we try to take care of them. We keep bird food out for them, as well."

"Really?" Minnie moved closer. "If I was a bird, I would never fly away. I would just let you feed me all the time."

Calhoun laughed, adjusting a wire that a birdhouse hung from. "Now, if you'll notice," he began, "this house is empty. But in a couple of weeks, we may find something totally different."

"You'll have to write us and tell us," Kenny said.

Calhoun hesitated. "Right. Now in the interest of birdie friends everywhere, we only rent these apartments out because we know if we don't, they'll create their own place to live and make a mess, or they'll simply keep flying, looking for the perfect spot. We think we have the perfect spot right here."

He leaned out to adjust one of the squash-shaped houses, his hand missed, his boot slipped on the rung, and before he knew it, Calhoun slid down the ladder, pinwheeling his arms until he hit the ground.

"You're hurt!" Minnie exclaimed, grinning down into his face. "Calhoun! You're hurting!"

"Yes, I am," he choked out. "It could be any number of things, but I'm starting with general misery."

Kenny clapped his hands. "This is the best!" Then he peered closely at Calhoun. "Is anything broken?"

"Maybe my spirit," Calhoun said.

"Is it the Curse?" Minnie whispered.

"The Curse?" Calhoun frowned, trying to concentrate, realizing he was out in the back fields with two kids who were too young to be around a groaning man.

"The Curse of the Broken Body Parts," she said reverently. "I prayed that's what you'd get for Christmas."

"And I thank you," Calhoun said, grunting as he tried to focus on his fingers. Still on his hand. Check. "But there's no such thing. It's just a silly superstition. And it's completely unnecessary for you to waste your Christmas prayers on me." He groaned longer for sympathy and also to make certain he still could. God, the pain left him breathless.

"Christmas prayers are never a waste, Calhoun. Try to sit up. Or do you want to cry first?"

"Cry first," Calhoun said. "Give me ten minutes to adjust my wits."

"I bet none of your brothers ever fell out of a tree," Kenny said admiringly. "That was like a swan dive."

Calhoun's eyes felt as if they were spinning in his head. "Do swans dive? I'm thinking no."

Minnie patted his hand. "Do you want us to go get Gypsy?"

"Gypsy?"

"Yes," Minnie said. "She can drag you home."

"No, thanks. I just want to lie here for a minute and let the clouds roll by, accompanied by the sweet choral music in my head."

Kenny patted his shoulder. "When we prayed, we prayed you'd only get hurt a little. Just enough to make The Curse work."

"There's no such thing as a curse," Calhoun said. "Well, there might be, but it's statistically unproven. It's a theoretical thing. Or maybe it's statistically proven, but not verified by an independent counsel."

"Gosh," Minnie said. "I don't think this worked," she told Kenny. "He was supposed to get hurt and fall in love with Momma. He's yakking, but not about her."

"Hmm," Calhoun said. "You kids have been working on me. I'll have to keep an eye on you in the future. You're regular little voodoo-meisters. Witch doctors."

"Kenny wants to be a doctor when he grows up."

"Yeah? What do you want to be?"

Minnie smiled. "A mother. And a horse trainer."

He closed his eyes. "I can see you being a mother. Be a horse trainer first." He sighed. "You know, I fell because I thought I saw my brother Last."

Kenny giggled. "In the tree?"

"No." Calhoun took stock of his body parts again. "I thought I saw a motorcycle drive up, and I quit paying attention to my footing, and down I went."

For a moment, he closed his eyes, then opened them again. When he could focus, he saw Last's face peering down at him. It looked like Last, only the earring was gone and the hair looked right. There were no visible tattoos, scars or bones through the nose. Calhoun moaned. "I *am* seeing things. Kids, maybe you better go get your mom or one of my brothers."

"What are you doing lying down on the job, Calhoun?" Last asked.

"Did I just hear my little brother speak? Minnie, is there a Jefferson hanging over my face?"

"Yes," she said, "you're not imagining things."

"How can you tell it's a Jefferson?" He wanted to be sure in case he was hearing things, too.

"He looks like you. And he gave us peppermints."

"Calhoun, can you sit up?" Last asked.

"I don't know as I care to. If you truly are you, what are you doing back so soon?"

"I have a baby being born. Jefferson men always look after their responsibilities."

Maybe it was Last with a brain transplant. "Your baby was already born. Yesterday. Congratulations, it's a girl named Annette. She has a bald head, rubbery lips and eyes so big she looks like an alien. I suspect those attributes will help her take a beauty-queen crown in a pageant someday."

"She's not supposed to arrive until tomorrow," Last said.

"Annette is a punctual lass. I predict she will always be early, but never Last." Calhoun smirked, pleased with himself.

"Look, Calhoun. I think you may have rung your bell just a bit. Can you sit up or do you need me to get the boys?"

"You can get the boys," Calhoun said. "I'll just lie here like a good sacrifice."

"Yeesh, he thinks he's a comedian when his brain's bumping around inside his skull. Kids, will you sit right here and make sure he doesn't wander off?"

Minnie giggled. "He's not that bad."

Kenny dutifully waved his hand over Calhoun's face.

"I'll be right back."

"That's not what you said before," Calhoun protested. "Before, you said you didn't know when you'd be back. That's not my brother. It's an impostor. An impostor!" He looked at the children. "Was my brother just here?"

"Mr. Calhoun," Minnie said, "could you try to be quiet for just a few minutes? As Momma sometimes tells us, 'I need to empty out my ears, children, and you keep fillin' 'em back up.'"

"Sure," Calhoun said on a sigh.

"ONLY A SLIGHT CONCUSSION," Doc Gonzalez said a few hours later, after the Jefferson boys had come galloping out to where Kenny and Minnie sat keeping watch over Calhoun. They'd picked him up gently and carried him sacrifice-style—his word, not theirs—to a truck. Then they'd sent Minnie and Kenny to the house to be with their mother and taken Calhoun to the hospital for a scan. "He'll be right as rain in a few days. No strenuous activity for a couple days, though."

"Thanks, Doc," Mason said. "Let's haul him home."

"What do we do with him, then?" Archer asked.

"Calhoun, you have two choices," Mason said. "You can stay at the main house, and Helga will look in on you when she has time. Or you can stay in the second house, and be a part of the little family you brought home for the holidays."

"I'll go with the little family I brought home for the holidays. At least I'll get some peace and quiet," Calhoun said. "And while we're all here, I propose a family caucus."

No one said anything. Doc edged to the door. "I'll

just be seeing patients. If anyone needs anything short of stitches, call me."

"Mason, Mimi's selling her place," Calhoun said from his perch on the examining table.

"What?" Mason exclaimed. "What are you smokin'?"

"Nothing." Calhoun gingerly sat up. "Not smoking anything, and my head's not swimming with little birdies anymore. Someone back me up here."

The brothers all silently nodded, except Last.

"I don't understand," Mason said. "How can she sell her family home?"

"Because life goes on," Calhoun told him. "We all need to get better with our adjustment cycles." He took a deep breath. "Now the really bad news. Olivia's mother is Marvella."

"That is bad news," Last said. "That's worse news than when I got Valentine pregnant. That was just a plot I succumbed to. You're actually considering bringing Marvella into the family *tree.*"

"Thank you, Last, for your support," Calhoun said on a growl.

Mason crossed his arms. "It is bad luck," he said, "but I don't see what difference it makes."

"You don't?"

"No." Mason rubbed at his chin. "It may even come to some good. She may have some loyalty inside her somewhere. We absorbed Valentine into the family. It may be a bit harder, but I'm sure we can absorb Marvella, as well."

"Dude, can you imagine her sitting down to Christmas dinner with us?" Crockett demanded.

"Yegods," Calhoun said. "I don't know that I've thought that far ahead. I just wanted to get the confession out of the way. And I think the concussion moved the confession schedule up by about a week, because I'm pretty certain I hadn't planned on dealing with this today."

"Speaking of Christmas dinner, did anyone get an invitation out to Hawk and Jellyfish?" Mason asked. "Those two are just as much a part of the family as the girls from the Union Junction Salon. And did we invite Delilah and the Lonely Hearts girls?"

"Did we order extra help for Helga?" Calhoun said on a grunt.

"There's all of us, and I figure Olivia will be happy to help. Are you sure Mimi's selling her place?" Mason asked. "This could be our last Christmas together."

"Oh, boy. Who's got diarrhea of the mouth now?" Calhoun asked, sliding off the table. "I need to empty out my ears," he said, quoting Olivia's kids. "Don't freak, Mason. She's just moving into town."

"But that's not the same. And people just don't sell their family home."

"They do when they have to. Mimi's going to finish her father's term as sheriff and then run for the office herself. She can't do that and take care of her farm and take care of him. It makes sense," Calhoun said, cramming his feet into his boots. "I wish everything made as much sense as Mimi." He sighed. "I'm heading down the hall to visit Valentine and Annette, and then I want to be taken to my lodge where my squaw and her papooses can treat me like a chief."

"Yeah, buddy," Archer said, "he only lost about a billion brain cells with that swan dive from space."

"I heard that," Calhoun said, "and until I can think more clearly, the family conference is adjourned. I've got a baby to hold."

Chapter Sixteen

Olivia watched as Calhoun casually strolled into the house, followed by his brothers. "I'm fine," he said, holding up a majestic hand before he went upstairs.

His brothers looked at her apologetically. "Can you take care of him until his wits are unscrambled? It shouldn't take long since it's only a slight concussion," Mason said. "Shouldn't is the operative, but perhaps dicey, word. He seems to be channeling some ego-driven ghost from our family's past."

"It's their fault," Calhoun called down the stairs. "The kids wanted me banged up. So here I am."

Olivia smiled. "Sure. He and Dad can keep each other company."

The brothers left, after glancing one more time at the ceiling. Before he left, Mason whispered, "He'll be fine soon, but for the moment, he's having delusions of grandeur."

"No royalty here," she assured Mason. "I'll let the kids take care of him."

Mason nodded, tipped his hat and left.

"Olivia!" Calhoun called. "Where are the kids?"

She went halfway up the stairs. He came to the landing.

"They're at the main house, making cookies with Helga."

"Where's your father?"

"He went with the kids, then apparently took some stuff over to Mimi's house for Helga, met the sheriff and decided to sit and have an old man's chat. At least that's how he referred to it when he called here a moment ago to check in. How do you feel?"

"Like I had a watermelon dropped on my head. Splitting sort of headache. Doc says it'll pass. It sure doesn't feel like a mild concussion, though."

"Go to sleep," she told him. "Did they give you any painkillers?"

"No. They want you to watch me in case I start getting sick, or a bit clueless, or whatever. Changes in my personality."

"They want me to watch you?"

Calhoun nodded. "Doc said someone had to do it. Your children prayed for me to get hurt, so the Curse of the Broken Body Parts would be visited upon me. I'm hurt, so now I'm here."

Olivia nodded. "Okay. See that room at the top of the stairs that has a bass over the door?"

He glanced over his shoulder. "Yes. It's my room."

"Excellent. Go in there, shut the door, turn out the light and snuggle up in your bed. I'm going to stay down here and fix some supper for my clan."

He frowned. "Don't you want to eat at the big house?"

"Well, it's nice, Calhoun, but Helga shouldn't have to take us on unexpectedly."

"You're Jefferson guests. She'll think you don't like her cooking. All Jefferson guests eat at the main house."

Olivia shook her head. "Kenny and Minnie are up there eating more cookies than they bake, I'm sure. Helga will know we just need our family time down here."

"If you say so. But I don't like it," he said.

"Well, we're not going to have any opinionated moments that we blame on our concussion," Olivia said lightly. "Your brother warned me that you might get a bit lippy."

"Ha! Don't you listen to anything my brothers say, especially not Mason! If he wasn't such a turtle, he'd have married the woman he loves instead of watching her move away!"

Olivia walked back down the stairs. "Go rest. I've got things to do."

"Aren't you concerned that your children specifically prayed for me to get hurt for Christmas? So that The Curse would work?"

"Yes, I am, actually. I'll talk to them about it," Olivia said. "They should never want someone to get hurt."

"That's not exactly the point," Calhoun said. "In my family, we tease that we haven't fallen…oh, never mind."

"Go to bed. I'll check on you in an hour and make certain you're not 'stupid,' as you suggested."

Calhoun watched Olivia walk away, then heard her go into the kitchen. Maybe The Curse wasn't a curse. Falling out of a tree was just plain falling out of a tree, then. He'd have to tell Minnie that he'd been wrong; The Curse, which could actually be considered a blessing, was truly only a superstition.

"I don't suppose you want to check on me from the close proximity of my bed?" he called.

"No! Go to sleep!"

"Spoken to just like a little kid," he grumbled. "Stupid curse isn't worth a flip!"

THANK HEAVENS Mason had warned her not to listen to anything that came out of Calhoun's mouth! If she didn't know better, she'd think he was trying to sweet-talk her.

Apparently, not only did you have to watch out for cowboys, but cowboys with concussions were particularly to be avoided!

As she chopped peppers, she thought about what it would be like if she and Calhoun were married. She thought about her last name being changed to Jefferson. "Olivia Jefferson," she murmured. "Ew, that would make my initials OJ, like orange juice. I'd have to stick with Spinlove. Spinlove-Jefferson. That might work."

Very long and complicated, though. Good thing they'd understood that neither of them was trying to make anything permanent out of their association, since everything about the two of them seemed to turn out long and complicated.

Except their lovemaking. That had been long and wonderful.

Calhoun came into the kitchen. "I thought about calling for a glass of water," he said, walking by her in nothing more than a pair of faded blue jeans. "But I decided I could yell myself hoarse and just make myself thirstier before you'd come to my aid."

Olivia quickly turned her head, chopping furiously. He had no shirt on and was barefoot. His jeans were low and casually tight to his body. He acted as if it was nothing to walk into a kitchen half-naked!

She heard him fill up a glass from the fridge, then he stood there and drank it, his back to her as if she weren't there. Sneaking a quick peek, Olivia got an eyeful of broad back as he lifted the glass to his mouth. Calhoun in broad daylight was even better than Calhoun by moonlight in a trailer!

She went back to chopping furiously.

"You like your peppers chopped fine," he said, suddenly beside her. "Are you making a paste?"

"It's for meat loaf," she said stiffly.

"Hmm. Sounds good. I like my meat loaf with just a bit of crunch," he said. "That, I would have to say, is pretty close to puree. I bet it will still be good, though."

"No doubt," she said between clenched teeth. "For a man who's just had his head scanned, you're awfully peppy."

"Well, the action appears to be down here. Can I help you?"

"No. No, thank you."

He moved her hair back behind her ear. "Is something wrong? I seem to be on the receiving end of some bad karma with you lately."

She laid the knife down, turning to face him. "Calhoun, we agreed we weren't going to be anything except acquaintances, particularly for the week I'm here. I'm not going to take advantage of being on your ranch to make a play for you. I'd appreciate you not hitting on me in my kitchen."

"Your kitchen?" he said lazily.

"My kitchen," she emphasized. "Because you invited me to stay here, and so here we are, but just because I'm cooking doesn't mean I'm trying to stir up your sauce."

"Mason didn't care about Marvella being your mother," he said. "I wish I hadn't let it throw me. I think I hurt your feelings, Olivia."

"You did." She turned back to her work, beginning to chop mushrooms. "It threw me, and it upset me, and that was the last thing I ever expected anyone to say to me when my father was in the hospital. I was worried sick about him! And then this strange woman says 'I'm your mother,' like she said, 'Here are flowers for your father,' and then she walked out of my life the same way she walked in. Nonchalant, like it didn't mean a damn thing. I could have used some support about then," she said angrily, "but what I got from you instead was the big hands-off, because I might mean trouble to the family. And you know what? I'm from a family where loyalty means everything, Calhoun. I totally understand family." She shrugged at him. "But I wouldn't cut other people out like they didn't matter, then expect them to come back when I changed my mind."

"It scared me, Olivia. I can apologize. But we just had a baby born yesterday who was the focal point of a lawsuit from Marvella. She tried to get to us through an employee's child. How much easier would I make it for her if I fell in love with her daughter?"

"I'm not asking you to change your feelings, Calhoun. I'm just saying don't ask me to run into your arms now that your family has given you the green light." She paused, looking at him. "I'm not going to lie and say that I don't care about you. I'm not going to deny that a part of me fantasized about the two of us, and maybe still does. But the strong part of me, the wise part, knows that you'd always be looking past me for Marvella. You'd never trust me. I had a marriage where there was no trust. I know nothing lasts that way."

"You still live in the past," he told her.

"Yes. And so do you. Only I didn't need my family to give me permission to love, Calhoun. My father was against you, and I still was crazy for you. I made love with you. So maybe someday your family decides they don't like me. Then I'm out. Well, that's not love. Love is two people."

Calhoun stared at her. "Olivia, I'm pretty new at this love thing, I'll admit. I know I made a mistake."

"Yeah. You did. You romanced my kids, you romanced me, my horse, you even got my father's respect. But what you didn't do was fall in love with me. You fell for everything around me, but not me. Once you found out who I really was, you vamoosed. I can live with that. I just think you should, too."

Calhoun stared at Olivia, his heart beating uncomfortably hard. She was telling him there was no chance for them to move forward. As far as she was concerned, there was no them. They were finished.

He didn't know what else to say.

"Don't come in here," she said softly, "and tell me that just because my kids prayed for some silly curse to work, and you took a bump on the head, that I am the woman for you. That's just an excuse to say what you should have said before. I'm a grown woman, Calhoun, and next time I fall for a man, he's going to be a man. Not a little boy who needs voodoo or some other silliness to admit his feelings."

Calhoun swallowed. "I hardly know what to say to such a steamed-up little woman. I sort of sense that anything I say right now isn't going to cut it. So I think I'll head upstairs and watch *Oprah* and hope my concussion doesn't kill me."

"Good idea," she said tightly. "I already have two children and a sick father to care for. They come first, Calhoun. They're my family."

"I got it, I got it," he said, backing out of the

kitchen with his hands in the air in mock surrender. "No nooky on the kitchen table when I'm concussed. No naked-Olivia-cooking-my-dinner fantasy when I've just gotten out of the hospital. And especially no chocolate-and-strawberries sex on the kitchen floor when I've just fallen out of a tree teaching your kids about bird feeders."

"Calhoun," she said, her tone warning.

"I got it," he said. "I'm gone."

He left, then peeked back around the corner. "I thought I saw potential weakening in your stance when I mentioned chocolate—"

"You didn't," she assured him. "Figment of your imagination."

"Just checking." Whew. This was no woman you cajoled out of a bad mood. He obviously couldn't tease Olivia into a good humor.

The problem was, she had a point. He had moved back about ten yards when he'd found out about Marvella. Now he was relying on humor to smooth over what wasn't funny—a very boyish maneuver. "Grade school," he muttered. "Like tugging on a girl's pigtails and being mean when really you just want her to like you."

That wasn't going to cut it with Olivia.

Frankly, it shouldn't.

He was really messing up. Olivia might not believe in charms and curses, but one thing he did believe in stoutheartedly was that no man let a good thing get away from him if he really wanted it.

It was time to get smart.

He put on a shirt, combed his hair, brushed his teeth and put on some cologne. Boots were required for serious conversations, so he pulled those on, too.

Maybe flowers.

No, not flowers. It was December, and all he had around was a poinsettia, and he wasn't going to hold out a potted poinsettia.

Taking a deep breath, he went downstairs and into the kitchen.

But Olivia wasn't in there. The pot was empty and washed out. Peppers no longer lay on the cutting board, and that had been washed clean, too.

That was a very bad sign from a woman who claimed this domain as her own.

"Olivia!" he called, his heart beginning to race. "Olivia!

There was no answer, so he ran outside. The motor home was still parked outside, which eased his mind a bit.

Banging on the door, he breathed even easier when Olivia opened it.

"Olivia," he said. "I was…what are you doing?"

"I prefer to live in my own home," she told him. And then she closed the door.

Chapter Seventeen

Olivia closed her eyes, then peeked to see if Calhoun was walking away. He was, and she relaxed slightly.

Gosh, he'd looked handsome. Smelled so good.

She'd wanted to drag him into the trailer for a repeat of their lovemaking.

But sex wasn't enough to build a lasting relationship on. She knew that too well.

Whether it was more than sex, they would never know. Marvella's words had proven prophetic, because even if she didn't come between them as far as Calhoun was concerned, she did as far as Olivia was concerned.

Banging on her door startled her again. She opened it.

Calhoun stood outside holding a potted poinsettia. "I know I said beware the dragon bearing gifts, but I should also confess. Beware the ogre bearing gifts."

"Now that's more like it," she said, opening the

door to take the poinsettia. Then she let the screen door swing closed again.

"No invitation in?"

"No ogres allowed in my house. They mess up the carpet."

He frowned. "Olivia, we need to talk."

"I'm listening."

A sigh escaped him. "I messed up," he said simply. "And I have the worst feeling that you're a high-risk kind of girl, and if I don't tell you everything I should, I'll wake up tomorrow morning and your motor home will be gone."

"I was considering that," she said, "but my kids are enjoying being here. I'm not going to steal their vacation time away from them."

He nodded. "Could we start over?"

"No. There are no do-overs in romance. You may have had part of your brain jangled by falling out of a tree, but my memory is perfectly fine."

"I don't want to lose you," he said, "because everything in my life changed when I met you."

She stared at him.

"For the better," he said. "Everything about you feels like home to me."

"Calhoun, I don't want to be your home. I want to be your raging passion, like your artwork, and I want to be your friend, and I want to be your one-time show."

"Of course I meant all that, but I didn't want to scare you," Calhoun said. "I'm trying to take it easy on the stuff that seems cheesy. You know, like you really make me horny, and when I shave, I think about your breasts, and when I eat, I think about that curve of your behind, and when I'm putting out food for the dog, I lose my breath because I start thinking about that tiny little freckle on your third rib—"

"Calhoun, that's a birthmark, not a tiny freckle."

"No bigger than my pinkie," he said. "That's tiny."

He had pretty big hands. Olivia figured he was doing his best to say that her birthmark was just a freckle in his eyes. She sighed. "I must admit I think about your love handles," she said.

"I do not have love handles!"

"And I think about your beer belly," she continued, "and the loose skin under your eyes, and your bald spot—"

He tore the screen open and grabbed her, kissing her until her breath left her. "You think about me," he said, "because I gave you a rousing good time in bed. You think about me, Olivia Spinlove, because I love your kids, I honor your father and your horse digs my act. I appreciate your being in a snit over the whole Marvella thing, but now you're holding it between us, which is exactly what she wants you to do, and so she wins. But you know something, Olivia? No one, including her, has ever beaten me at anything that mattered." And he kissed her again, making her knees weak and her heart race before he set her away from him.

"Think about that," he said, "while you're deciding about playing hard to get. Think about my lie-detector test and tell me you could pass if I asked you if you love me. I don't think you want to give me up, Ms. Spinlove. I sure as shooting don't want to give you up, because you're the only woman who's ever, ever knocked my mind off of my nudes. All I ever wanted to do was paint nudes that Michelangelo would admire. Breasts Botticelli would praise. Hips that Renoir would swoon—"

"I think I get your drift," Olivia said, interrupting. "You forgot all about nudes when you met me."

"Well, I didn't forget about one nude. And when a man can't get his mind off of one special nude, then he best take stock of his situation. I took stock of mine, and I think you should make your family mine and vice versa."

Olivia blinked. "I know you're not proposing, because Helga said that every Jefferson male who'd ever gotten married had to leave the ranch to be with his true love. She said it was getting pretty tight around here and that she'd cut down her weekly grocery list."

"I took a header out of a tree for you," Calhoun said. "Could that count?"

"I don't think so," Olivia said.

"Are you saying you'd accept a proposal?"

She wasn't falling for that. "Calhoun, you cannot have it both ways. You can't prepropose on condition of knowing the outcome."

He studied her. "Just checking."

So? Was he proposing? She didn't think so. Somewhere in here, she felt a Jefferson hook. One had to be very careful, she'd learned, when dealing with these men.

"I wasn't proposing, anyway," he said.

"I didn't get the impression you were, cowboy," she said mildly. "I would guess preproposals don't often pan out. Sort of like looking for gold in your backyard pond."

"Actually," he said, brightening, "there was talk that on Widow Fancy's farm—" He looked at her and hesitated. "Never mind."

"Never mind what?"

"Just never mind."

He strode away. "Just like that," she murmured. "One second he's talking about proposals, and the next he's talking about Widow Fancy, and then he's slipped away. Good thing Mason warned me about his state of mind, because he very nearly changed mine!"

IT WAS THE MEMORY of Widow Fancy's rumored Civil War gold that made Calhoun remember his father's sage advice: *The treasure lies within.*

If there was treasure, he needed to make certain he didn't end up with fool's gold. And that meant running the proper checks to make certain his exploration was on target.

Olivia didn't seem interested in preproposals, but a smart man didn't waste time gambling.

He was pretty certain that if he did everything right, he wouldn't be coming up with a dry well.

At the house, he found Kenny and Minnie, baking with Helga. They had flour on their faces and cookie dough in their hair.

"Miss Helga is good to you, isn't she?" he asked the children.

They loved Miss Helga. He could tell by the light in their eyes as they gazed up at her. So much attention she wanted to give them.

So much attention Kenny and Minnie were willing to soak up.

So much attention *he* wanted to give them, too. And he wanted theirs, even when he was getting thrown from a bull or bungee jumping without a bungee. What would he do without hearing their little voices call, "Calhoun!"

"Hey," he said to them, "I had an idea. I wanted to run it past you, since you're the minds behind the show."

"Okay," Minnie said.

"I was wondering," Calhoun said, drawing them to him, "I was wondering if you ever thought about having a...you know. A father."

Minnie's eyes grew round. "We *thought* about it," she said, "we just don't think Momma's ever going to say yes. We've given up," she announced.

"Totally?"

"Totally," Minnie said. "Right, Kenny?"

He nodded, the lock of hair Minnie called his bird perch sticking straight up out of his crown.

"If she said yes to me, would you like having me for a dad?"

Minnie and Kenny stared at him silently.

"Well, don't be in a hurry to say yes," he said.

"We're not," Minnie said. "We're thinking."

"You're always thinking," Calhoun said. "When I become your father, you're going to start acting like a little girl. And you, Kenny, are going to learn to be a little boy. You're going to know the meaning of childhood."

"And I'm going to have a dress," Minnie said, "a pretty one with lace and ruffles—"

"And I'm going to have, to have…" Kenny said, trying to keep up.

"A Sunday suit," Minnie said, "to match my dress. And ribbons in my hair. And Kenny gets Sunday-best boots and a real haircut. Not Momma mowing his head with Grandpa's old—"

"Yes," Calhoun said. "All that. No more thinking and worrying, though. You leave that to the adults, until you're old enough to worry. Maybe fifteen is appropriate. I think seventeen's about when we started. I'll ask Mason," he said, thinking.

"In that case, we accept," Minnie said. "You can try to talk a yes out of Mom, but we suggest you have two plans because she'll probably have a no for you right out of the chute. That's what we do."

"Yes, I know," Calhoun said, "and from now on, yes means yes, and no means no, and there's going to be no second plans. If I become your father, that is."

Minnie sighed. "You drive a hard bargain, cowboy. We'll sharpen our negotiating skills."

He tugged her hair and ruffled Kenny's. "Come on, then. We've got chores to do."

"Okay. Bye, Helga!" they said.

She hugged them and handed Calhoun a gingerbread man.

"Thank you," he said.

She nodded.

"All right. Do you know where your grandfather is?"

"He was with the sheriff, but then he said he was going to go down and chat with Gypsy."

"Sounds good. Now this is the hard part—"

"Not really," Minnie said. "He'll say yes."

"How do you know?" Calhoun asked, surprised.

"We heard him telling the sheriff that he figured you weren't as bad as he thought you were. And the sheriff said there were no finer men, once they found the right woman. No card cheating, no drinking, no whor—"

"Whoa, that's plenty," Calhoun said. "Thanks. How long were you standing outside the door?"

"Long enough to hear the sheriff go south of good manners," Minnie said, "and that's when we knew Grandpa had found a friend."

Suddenly, she stopped. Kenny stood beside her. "Calhoun, if you and Momma get married...will we live here, on the road, or in Kansas?"

"I don't know," he said honestly. "Which would you prefer?"

"I don't know, either," she said. "This is nice, but I sort of miss the show. And Kansas is home. What do you think, Kenny?"

He shrugged. "I don't care. Long as I can keep Gypsy."

"Oh, Gypsy. Gypsy is…Gypsy is part of the family," Calhoun said.

"Momma would never get rid of Gypsy," Minnie said to Kenny. "It's catching and keeping Calhoun we gotta worry about."

"Exactly my thought," Calhoun said.

THIRTY MINUTES LATER, Calhoun had asked and received permission to propose to Olivia. It was, as the kids had said, the simple part.

The hard part was taking care of the deal maker.

"Which one?" he asked the children.

Their eyes were huge, as was his, as they stared into the jeweler's case. He could never have imagined that engagement rings came in so many styles. He had no idea what Olivia would want. Diamonds, pearls, emeralds, sapphires. Big, little, solitaire, heart shaped, round or square? Flaws? The four Cs?

He was totally confused.

"That one," Minnie said, her face wreathed in a big smile.

"Which one?" he asked.

She pointed to a ring that had three diamonds across. Kenny bobbed his head in agreement. The diamonds were a fair size, he thought, and feminine and deliciously round, reminding him somehow of Olivia's nipples. How could that be? Was that a good thing? Would she be offended?

He decided he wouldn't tell her. Because, after all, he was a man who saw beauty in a woman's body—and hers was the only body he ever cared to see for the rest of his life. So if he saw her body when he saw beautiful things, then that just meant his eyes would always be full of her.

"We'll take it," he said. "Excellent choice, children. This one's a keeper, I can tell."

"THIS HAS TO BE DONE just right," Minnie told Calhoun. "Try to be a little more still."

She flattened his hair with water from the sink. "I'm not spit-combing you," she told him.

"Thank you," he said dryly.

Kenny beamed. "It works good, though."

Minnie had on a beautiful new dress. Lots of ruffles. A pretty cherry-fuchsia that complemented her skin and would be perfect to wear to church on Christmas Eve. Plus, she had pretty stockings and a pair of shiny black shoes with bows on top. Calhoun had worried about the bows—maybe Olivia would think they were too fancy—but Minnie had been so agog over the tiny heels and the bows he couldn't say no.

Kenny wore a pair of charcoal slacks, a white button-down shirt, a blue blazer and a tie he'd picked out himself. The tie was green and printed with red candy canes and holly, and it made Calhoun's eyes twirl to look at it, but it was Kenny's first tie, and Calhoun figured a boy's tie ought to be a real positive experience. Kenny also had on black boots with gray pulls and toes, because Calhoun had told him he couldn't have the ones with silver toes. That, he said, could come on his sixteenth birthday—wherever he was, he promised.

It was a bit too fancy for Calhoun, but when Kenny chose the black-and-gray boots, he knew they'd come to the perfect compromise. Kenny looked so grown-up, and he knew it.

Then Calhoun had taken the children to the Union Junction Salon, and let the ladies fuss over their hair. Lily had put so many ringlets in Minnie's hair she looked like a princess.

Kenny, for once, had a manly, clean style. Just like a prince, Calhoun figured.

"All that's missing now is Gypsy," Minnie told him. "Let's go before Momma starts looking for us."

They got Gypsy from the pasture and put a saddle on her. She seemed to know something was up because she began putting on her show airs, prancing her way over to the motor home.

At the door, Calhoun gave her the command to tap.

Gypsy went tap-tap-tap! with her hoof, the way she did on Grandpa's barrels.

Olivia came to the door with her hair wrapped in a towel and wearing a bathrobe. The minute she saw Calhoun with Minnie and Kenny in front of him on Gypsy, all dressed in their finery, she started to cry. And laugh.

She ran out the door and flung her arms around Gypsy's neck. Calhoun got off the horse and went down on bended knee. Olivia hugged his neck, and Gypsy stuck her nose over his shoulder.

"Olivia, I love you. I love you more than I've ever loved anything in my life. I love you. I love your children. I love the way you laugh. And I love the way you argue your point. I want you to marry me, and I want to be your husband. I'll do my best to be the best husband I know how to do. And when I mess up, I know you'll keep me straight. Olivia Spinlove, will you do me the honor of becoming my wife?" he asked.

Olivia was so happy she had tears pouring down her face.

"Give her the ring, Calhoun," Minnie whispered, and Gypsy gave him a nudge with her nose.

So he pulled out the ring box and handed it to Olivia.

She took it, her eyes on his, and at the last second, he snatched it back.

She looked at him.

"I'm not handing you a box," he said, "I'm handing you my heart." Taking the ring out, he slid it onto her finger himself. "Now you can decide if you like it, Olivia. Please say you'll have me."

The diamonds splashed fiery white ice at her. Olivia gasped. "It's the most beautiful ring I ever saw," she murmured. "Calhoun, I, it's too—"

"If you say yes, the cost was not too great," he said. "You and your family are worth more than any diamonds I could give you, Olivia. Three diamonds. You, and your two children. That's what I want."

She started to cry. "I love you, Calhoun. Yes. I would love to be your wife. I really would. I'm so happy, I think I'm going to cry!"

Minnie and Kenny began clapping their hands; Gypsy blew a loud nee-eeee! over Calhoun's shoulder. He pulled Olivia to her feet, and they went to stand beside the children, looking up at them so that Olivia could show the ring now that it was on her finger, and Grandpa sneaked up to take a few pictures of them as one big happy family.

It was the picture Calhoun and Olivia had dreamed of.

THREE WEEKS LATER, Christmas was a time of joy for the Jefferson family. Many blessings were showered on them, though they had felt near disaster not too many weeks before. When Frisco Joe, Laredo, Ranger, Tex and Fannin came home for Christmas that year, they were anxious to see the newest addition to the family, Annette.

They wanted to see Mason, back from his journey.

The sheriff felt better and was able to join them at the fireplace in the Jefferson's main house. Helga had decorated the tree beautifully, so that it was the best it had ever been. She had a way with making things lovely, and she worked her magic on her special Santa gifts for the brothers once again.

The brothers' plaid stockings hung down the staircase, as usual, only this year there was a difference: Helga had made new stockings for Frisco Joe and Annabelle's new baby, as well as little Emmie, Annette, Nanette, Minnie and Kenny. The new stockings, Minnie and Kenny were quick to note, were a bit larger and had their names in fancy glitter glue and embroidery.

They felt very much a part of the family.

Valentine was feeling well, and she had a permanent job offer waiting for her at the bakery in town.

Last's rebellious phase seemed to be gone, either from holding Annette or from having all twelve of the brothers back home and around the ranch once again.

The Lonely Hearts Salon and the Union Junction Salon stylists converged on the house on Christmas Eve night, invited by the Jeffersons, as was customary, but really with a mission that had all the women giggling upstairs, much to the curiosity of the men gathered downstairs.

Only Calhoun and Barley seemed to know what was afoot. The twinkle in Calhoun's eyes and the fine charcoal suit he was wearing should have been a giveaway to the brothers, but they were busy enjoying watching their wives getting to know each other and relaxing in the aura of being home once again.

But when Helga gathered everyone at the foot of the stairs, and Barley put on his best cowboy hat as he sat in a chair by the warmly glowing fireplace, and Lily began lightly playing a song that sounded familiar on a guitar, the brothers gathered around with smiles on their faces.

Minnie walked down the stairs, darling in a lace burgundy gown, a crown of baby's breath and shiny ribbons on her head. She tossed pink rose petals as she walked, and Calhoun's eyes glimmered with tears.

Kenny shyly made his way down the stairs, staring at Calhoun, in a suit and boots that matched Calhoun's. He looked quite serious, but he held the satin pillow with the rings on it quite firmly, and he stood beside the man who planned on adopting him and his sister.

And as Lily's guitar played in the background, Olivia came down the stairway, so much like an angel that Calhoun's Adam's apple jumped and his hands trembled. He couldn't believe that this woman was going to be his wife. She was so beautiful, and so right for him, that he could only thank heaven that her children had chosen him. Her long pink gown and delicate veil were the stuff of fairy tales. He was glad he'd insisted that she have this lovely dress, as he knew she'd had nothing like it before. This wedding, he'd told her, was going to be the wedding of her dreams.

And it was.

He looked down into Olivia's eyes and smiled. "I will love you all my life," he told her.

"I will love you all mine," she replied, her eyes sparkling at him.

When the sheriff proclaimed them married, Calhoun gathered Olivia to him, and then the children, and he cried for the treasure he'd been given. His father, Maverick, had said that the treasure was within; these three people would be within his heart for the rest of his life.

Bursting with happiness, Calhoun swept Olivia out the front door amid a shower of rose petals. They jumped into a carriage, pulled by a beribboned Gypsy, and they rode off into the evening under a big top of stars. The magically romantic night needed no applause.

Though Calhoun had started out with the goal of painting wonderful nudes and testing his manhood on a bounty bull, deep inside his heart he knew something else mattered more: family. No matter its shape or size, a family's happiness grew as each member changed themselves and therefore each other. The real treasure of family was within the bonds of love, despite the changes that came to every family.

So Calhoun, more than his brothers before him, embraced those changes when they happened. He just didn't know that the changes would be in the form of his new children.

Calhoun loved being a father.

Kenny and Minnie adored going to school in Union Junction. This is not to say that they didn't get into the occasional mischief, or sometimes forget their homework. In fact, they savored being the school-age children of the Jeffersons, whose reputation was well remembered. Kenny and Minnie best enjoyed snagging a ride into school on the back of Last's bike—very illegal, Last said, but they wore helmets he had made just for them. Or they rode in the truck of whichever brother was going into town. Most of all, they loved having all the houses to run between, as they visited the brothers, Helga, Mimi, the dog and the horses, where Gypsy fit right in. Calhoun threatened to put a satellite tracking device on the kids, but Olivia laughed and told him to relax. Malfunction Junction, she said, was a great place to be a kid.

Olivia's world was made complete by the fact that her father and Calhoun really did get along. Barley loved chatting with the sheriff, and Mimi's father enjoyed having a fellow "old-timer" around to play cards with. They compared their ailments and discussed the joys of being single fathers who raised strong-willed daughters. They even, on the sly, took to making bets on which brother would marry next. Barley used his flair for the dramatic and his way with words to become the spokesperson/sign-maker for Mimi's eventual run for sheriff. Barley sold his old farm with the windmill in Kansas, but Calhoun couldn't bear for his children not to have the one reminder of their Kansas home that they treasured.

He and his brothers went to Kansas and claimed the small windmill. He put it behind his and Olivia's new home, a gently turning backdrop that would always remind the children of their old home. Small mementos, Calhoun said, mattered most.

Best of all, Barley taught Calhoun everything he knew about being a rodeo clown, so twice a year the family went on the road performing. The kids had been right: Calhoun could run very fast. They loved this special time as a family, and Olivia was always grateful that, this time, she'd found a cowboy who understood that the glitter and glue of performing was nothing in her heart compared to the color he brought to her life.

Calhoun never did give up painting totally. He just turned his joy in the art to other mediums and styles and left the nudes behind. He finished the original portrait he'd painted of Kenny and Minnie and hung it in their bedroom, just for them to enjoy. They were, to Calhoun, much more beautiful in person, and that's how he preferred them.

The pictures Grandpa had snapped of them during Calhoun's proposal turned out to be the inspiration for Calhoun's greatest work of art. It was, he said, his Sistine chapel. He painted jeans and a pretty shirt on Olivia, and her hair as it normally was and not in a towel, but those were the only adjustments he made to the photograph of his favorite moment in time. The portrait of the four of them and Gypsy resided in the hallway of the home they made in Union Junction, just south of the three original homes at Malfunction Junction ranch. And every day when he came home and walked inside the house, the portrait brought him pride and peace.

But the original picture of the four of them with

Gypsy, the one with Olivia's hair in a towel, Calhoun put in a picture frame and kept on his desk, because that was how he loved his wife best—simply Olivia.

* * * * *

Don't miss the next rowdy romp from
Tina Leonard!
Turn the page for a sneak preview of
ARCHER'S ANGELS (AR #1053),
the latest book in the
COWBOYS BY THE DOZEN *miniseries!*
Available February 2005!

Prologue

Howdy, AussieClove.
What's shaking down under? I just got home from riding a bull at the rodeo in Lonely Hearts Station. After the events, me and some of my bros decided to drink some of the wildest concoction on the planet. We ended up baying at the moon beside Barmaid's Creek, with some crazy gals for company. You should have seen me ride that bull—if he hadn't come back around to the left, I would have been the first brother in my family to stay on that cursed piece of cowhide.
TexasArcher

G'day, TexasArcher.
Nothing shaking here except maybe my head. My sister Lucy is sad tonight. She and her husband have learned they can never have children. So I threw myself into work, hoping to stay positive.

The stunt tonight involved a boat, fire, a shark and two guys wearing what I would call thongs. I

think guys should never wear swim clothes that are smaller than their...well, you know. What do cowboys wear under those Wrangler jeans?
AussieClove

Man alive, AussieClove.
Sorry to hear about your sister—that's too bad. Around our ranch, we're having a population explosion. We've got babies popping out all over the place. I'm never having kids. In fact, I'm never getting married. Too complicated.

One time, I was stuck in a truck with my twin brother, Ranger, and his now-wife, Hannah, and they griped at each other for days. I finally escaped, but Ranger wasn't so lucky. He rolled down an arroyo and demanded that an Indian medicine man marry him and Hannah, because he was convinced he had to get married to live. My twin's weird.

By the way, I wear briefs and sometimes nothing. What do Aussie girls wear under their clothes? (I can tell you right now, floss-size drawers would never hold everything of mine.)
TexasArcher

Texas Archer
I'm sure. ☺
AussieClove

Turn the page for a preview of next month's American Romance titles!

We hope these brief excerpts will whet your appetite for all four of January's books...

One Good Man by Charlotte Douglas (#1049) is the second title in this popular author's ongoing series, "A Place to Call Home." Charlotte Douglas creates a wonderful sense of home and community in these stories.

Jeff Davidson eased deeper into the shadows of the gift shop. Thanks to his Special Operations experience, the former Marine shifted his six-foot-two, one-hundred-eighty pounds with undetectable stealth. But his military training offered no tactics to deal with the domestic firefight raging a few feet away.

With a stillness usually reserved for covert insertions into enemy territory, he peered through a narrow slit between the handmade quilts, rustic birdhouses, and woven willow baskets that covered the shop's display shelves.

On the other side of the merchandise in the seating area of the café, a slender teenager with a cascade of straight platinum hair yelled at her mother, her words exploding like a barrage from the muzzle of an M-16. "You are so not with it. Everyone I hang with has her navel pierced."

Jeff grimaced in silent disapproval. The kid should

have her butt kicked, using that whiny, know-it-all tone toward her mom. Not that the girl's behavior was his business. He hadn't intended to eavesdrop. He'd come to Mountain Crafts and Café to talk business with Jodie Nathan, the owner, after her restaurant closed. Lingering until the staff left, he'd browsed the shelves of the gift section until she was alone.

But before he could make his presence known, fourteen-year-old Brittany had clattered down the stairs from their apartment over the store and confronted her mother.

"Your friends' navels are their mothers' concern, not mine." The struggle for calm was evident in Jodie's firm words, and the tired slump of her pretty shoulders suggested she'd waged this battle too many times. "You are my daughter, and as long as you live under my roof, you will follow my rules."

Was the kid blind? Jeff thought with disgust. Couldn't she see the tenderness and caring in her mother's remarkable hazel eyes? An ancient pain gnawed at his heart. He'd have given everything for such maternal love when he'd been a child, a teenager. Even now. Young Brittany Nathan had no idea how lucky she was.

Daddy by Choice by Marin Thomas (#1050). A "Fatherhood" story with a western slant. This exciting new author, who debuted with the delightful *The Cowboy and the Bride*, writes movingly and well about parent-child relationships…and, of course, romance!

JD wasn't sure if it was the bright sunlight bouncing off the petite blond head or the sparkling clean silver rental car that blinded him as he swung his black Ford truck into a parking space outside Lovie's café. Both the lady and the clean car stood out among the dusty, mud-splattered ranch vehicles lined up and down Main Street in Brandt's Corner.

Because of the oppressive West Texas heat wave blanketing the area, he shifted into Park and left the motor running. Without air-conditioning, the interior temperature would spike to a hundred degrees in sixty seconds flat, and he was in no hurry to get out.

He had some lookin' to do first.

A suit in the middle of July? He shook his head at the blonde's outfit. Pinstripe, no less. She wore her honey-colored hair in a fancy twist at the back of her neck, revealing a clean profile. Evidently, she got her haughty air from the high cheekbones.

All of her, from her wardrobe to her attitude, represented a privileged life. Privileged meant money. Money meant trouble.

His gut twisted. Since yesterday's phone call from this woman, his insides had festered as if he'd swallowed a handful of rusty fence nails.

Fear.

Fear of the unknown…the worst kind. He'd rather sit on the back of a rank rodeo bull than go head to head with her. Too bad he didn't have the option.

Table for Five by Kaitlyn Rice (#1051) is an example of our "In the Family" promotion—stories about the joys (and difficulties) of life with extended families. Kaitlyn Rice is a talented writer whose characters will stay with you long after you've finished this book.

Kyle Harper glanced at his watch and uttered a mild curse. He'd worked well past a decent quitting time again—an old habit that was apparently hard to break. Shoving the third-quarter sales reports into his attaché case, he closed his eyes, claiming a few seconds of peace before switching gears. He pictured a perfect gin martini, a late version of the television news and a bundle of hickory wood, already lit and crackling in the fireplace.

Heaven.

Or home, as he'd once known it.

Life didn't slow down for hard-luck times, and it didn't cater to wealth or power. Kyle could afford only a moment to ponder used-to-be's. He popped open his eyes and grabbed his cell phone, the fumbling sounds at the other end warned him about what to expect. "Grab the guns!" Kyle's father yelled. "There's a gang of shoot-em-up guys headed into town!"

The Forgotten Cowboy by Kara Lennox (#1052). An unusual take on a popular kind of plot. Thanks to the heroine's amnesia, she doesn't recognize the cowboy in her life—which makes for some interesting and lively complications!

Willow Marsden studied the strange woman in her hospital room. She was an attractive female in her twenties, her beauty marred by a black eye and a bandage wound around her head. The woman looked unfamiliar; she was a complete stranger. Unfortunately, the stranger was in Willow's mirror.

She lay the mirror down with a long sigh. Prosopagnosia—that was the clinical name for her condition. She'd suffered a head injury during a car accident, which had damaged a very specific portion of her brain—the part that enabled humans to distinguish one face from another. For Willow, every face she saw was strange and new to her—even those of her closest friends and relatives.

"You're telling me I could be like this forever?"

Dr. Patel, her neurologist, shrugged helplessly. "Every recovery is different. You could snap back to normal in a matter of days, weeks, months, or…yes, the damage could be permanent."

"What about my short-term memory?" She couldn't even remember what she'd had for breakfast that morning.

Again that shrug. Why was it so difficult to get a straight answer out of a doctor?

Willow knew she should feel grateful to be alive, to be walking and talking with no disfiguring scars. Her car accident during last week's tornado had been a serious one, and she easily could have died if not for the speed and skill of her rescuers. Right now, though, she didn't feel grateful at all. Her plans and dreams were in serious jeopardy.

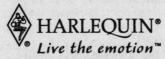

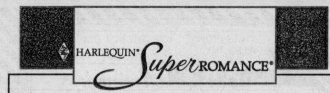

Mother and Child Reunion

A *ministeries* from
2003 RITA® finalist

Jean Brashear

Coming Home

Cleo Channing's dreams were simple: the stable home and big, loving family she never had as a child. Malcolm Channing walked into her life and swept her off her feet and before long, she thought she had it all—three beautiful children in a charming house she would fill to the rafters with love.

Their firstborn was a troubled girl, though, and the strain on their family grew until finally, there was nothing left to do but for them to all go their separate ways.

Now their daughter has returned, and as the days pass, awareness grows in Cleo and Malcolm that their love never truly died.

Except, the treacherous issues that drove them apart in the first place remain....

Heartwarming stories with a sense of humor, genuine charm and emotion and lots of family!

On sale starting January 2005
Available wherever Harlequin books are sold.

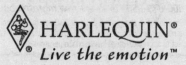

HARLEQUIN®
Live the emotion™

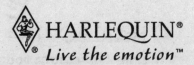

Forgotten Son by Linda Warren
Superromance #1250
On sale January 2005

Texas Ranger Elijah Coltrane is the forgotten son—the one his father never acknowledged. Eli's half brothers have been trying to get close to him for years, but Eli has stubbornly resisted. That is, until he meets Caroline Whitten, the woman who changes his mind about what it means to be part of a family.

By the author of *A Baby by Christmas* (Superromance #1167).

The Chosen Child by Brenda Mott
Superromance #1257
On sale February 2005

Nikki's sister survived the horrible accident caused by a hit-and-run driver, but the baby she was carrying for Nikki and her husband wasn't so lucky. The baby had been a last hope for the childless couple. Devastated, Nikki and Cody struggle to get past their tragedy. If only Cody could give up his all-consuming vendetta to find the drunk responsible—and make him pay.

Available wherever Harlequin books are sold.

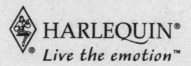